4 SLEUTHS & A BURLESQUE DANCER

A KILLER FOURSOME MYSTERY

LESLIE LANGTRY   ARLENE MCFARLANE

TRACI ANDRIGHETTI   DIANA ORGAIN

4 SLEUTHS & A BURLESQUE DANCER

A Killer Foursome Mystery

Copyright© 2022 by LMAO Press

ebook ISBN-13: 978-1-9994981-8-4
print ISBN: 978-1-9994981-9-1

Published by LMAO Press
Canada

Cover Design by Arlene McFarlane
Cover by Adrian Doan Kim

Formatting by Traci Andrighetti

❀ Created with Vellum

PROLOGUE

From: Kate Connolly
To: 4 Sleuths Group Chat

You guys! Jim surprised me with a trip to New Orleans. We're about to board a 6 p.m. flight! He rented us a house in the beautiful Garden District, so I'll have you all over tomorrow. The four of us will get to hang out again! This time in the lap of luxury.

FRANKI

TRACI ANDRIGHETTI

"Please, tell me I didn't hear you right, Kate." I squeezed my phone with one hand and gripped the edge of my desk at Private Chicks, Inc. with the other.

"You did."

"You're sure?"

"Dead certain."

Not an expression I would've used given our history, but okay.

Kate gave a flustered exhale. "The house Jim rented is owned by your landlady, Glenda O'Brien."

I released the desk and poured more Baileys Mudslide Coffee Creamer into my mug. The label promised a "whimsical spin" on my morning. Now I needed one. "What a small, twisted world."

"This is no coincidence. When I got back from Babette's bachelorette, Glenda came up in conversation. Unbeknownst to me, Jim contacted her, and she offered him this place at a steal—"

"As in, steal your money."

"We know that now, but he had no way of knowing that she's a slumlord."

"Too bad all the hotels are booked because of that hair show

Valentine and Merry are at." I sipped my coffee and waited for the whimsy. It didn't come. "Anyway, Glenda's not a slumlord. She's a sleazelord."

"What's the difference?"

"Um…things like pornographic wallpaper, condoms in the candy dish, a dining-room stripper pole…"

Kate gasped. "Is *that* what the pole in the entryway is for?"

I blinked. "What else?"

"It's by the stairs. I thought it might be a fire escape."

I put down my mug and the phone so I could massage my temples. Jim and Kate were going to have a hard time in The Big Easy. "I know San Francisco has the Tenderloin District and all, but New Orleans is a whole different animal."

"I'm seeing that. Cheetah, leopard, zebra, and tiger."

"She really went all out with the prints. The furnished apartment I rented sight unseen from her only has zebra and leopard." I spun my chair and looked out the window at Decatur Street in the French Quarter, three stories below. "Where is this place, anyway?"

"The Lower Garden District."

And I lived in a tiny dump in her fourplex in Uptown. I turned from the window and took a long sip from my mug. Still no whimsical spin. "The Lower Garden District isn't as fancy as the Upper Garden District, but it's still a wealthy neighborhood. And with all the restaurants, boutiques, and bars on Magazine Street, it's got character."

"Character is one way to describe this place."

"What's another?"

"A whorehouse version of the Park Avenue Hotel in Niagara Falls. You can't imagine it."

I grimaced. "Actually, I can. My place looks like a French brothel funeral parlor, and it comes with a creepy cemetery across the street."

"Gosh. How can you live there?"

"There's a great bar next to the cemetery."

"Oh. I sure wish I could drink. I could really use something stiff right now. Wait. No pun intended."

I leaned back in my chair. "Why don't I leave now to come meet you? By the time I check out the house and haggle with Glenda over your rental contract, it'll be time for Valentine and Merry's lunch break from the hair show."

"Jim and I would appreciate that, as long as it doesn't put you at odds with Glenda."

My landlady was a sixty-something ex-stripper, and I was a thirty-two-year-old PI who'd been thoroughly repressed by my Italian-Catholic family, so we were already as "at odds" as you could get. "Don't worry. I can handle her."

A buzz assailed my ears—and my brain. There was only one woman I couldn't handle, and I had to work with her, thanks to my kind-hearted fiancé.

"Franki," Kate said, "do you hear that buzzing sound?"

"Multiple times a day. It's Bradley's maniacal assistant."

"That's a relief. I was worried a forgotten sex toy had spontaneously turned on in the house."

"You're at Glenda's, so don't rule it out. See you in thirty." I hung up, grabbed my hobo bag, and charged the lobby.

Ruth Walker sat at the reception desk beside the office entrance. Despite her turkey neck, she looked like an angry ostrich with a tight graying-brown bun. She even had the facial fuzz.

I pulled back my long, brown hair, leaned all five-feet-ten of me into her space, and stared my cat-eyelined eyes into her cat-eye glasses. "What're you buzzing about now, woman?"

"Your 8:05 a.m. personal call." She gave me a blast of her so-called Get Busy Buzzer, and my fingers curled into turkey neck-wringing position.

Veronica Maggio, my best friend and boss, entered the main door in a crisp yellow linen dress that complemented her blonde hair and sunny disposition. Her cornflower blue eyes shifted from Ruth to me. "What's going on?"

I straightened my fingers. "I was about to remind Ruth that she doesn't run Private Chicks. *You* do."

Veronica picked up her mail from the desk. "She's right about that, Ruth. You work for Bradley."

Ruth was so mad, her turkey neck shook along with the chain hanging from her glasses. "And we all know the story of how he quit his cushy bank-president job for *this one here*"—she jerked her thumb at me—"which meant I got the boot in the process. Then *she* cost me my cruise-director job on the Galliano steamboat, too."

"You cost yourself that job," I said, "and then you barged in here and made a job for yourself. So what are you complaining about?"

"Your 8:05 a.m. personal call." She reached for the buzzer as her *Judge Judy* ringtone sounded. As a diehard devotee of the judge and all things justice, she put on her "listening ears" and grabbed her phone. "Lucky for you, missy, my boss is calling."

"Lucky for you, buzzy, my boss is right here." I took a step forward. "Otherwise, I'd stick that buzzer—"

Veronica took my hand. "Can I see you in my office?"

Without a word, I let her pull me back down the hall to the office next to mine. Before she could go on the offense, *I* did. First, I wrestled my arm free so I could flail it. "What are you going to do about Ruth Buzzi out there?"

She took a seat in the fuchsia leather chair behind her desk. "Ruth is Bradley's assistant, Franki. There's nothing I *can* do about her."

"But she's usurping your authority."

"She's trying to keep her boss on task."

"Yeah, all task and no me. She's the reason he's in Chicago right now. She convinced him he had to do some investigative work that he could've done from here."

Veronica ran a letter opener through an envelope. "You'll have to take that up with him. In the meantime, try to keep the peace."

"I was!" I gave a furious flail. "Then she started blasting that blasted buzzer."

"Ruth can be annoying, but she's been doing a great job. She and Bradley have been solving a lot of fraud cases. You have to admit, she's got a sharp eye for a scam."

"Because she's good at running them."

"Oh, Franki. She's harmless."

I threw up my arms. "Why do people always overlook the fact that ostriches and turkeys are fierce animals?"

Veronica puckered and set the letter opener and envelope on her desk. "Listen, it's been quiet around here—"

"Has it? With that buzzer?"

She licked her pink-glossed lips. "What I meant was, since you're between cases, why don't you take the rest of the day off? You said your friends were coming to town. You could show them around and blow off some steam."

"You got the steam part right. It's a sauna out there. But don't say *blow*."

"Why not?"

I parked my hands on my hips to prevent further flails. "You didn't see how pregnant Kate was last month, and those twins have been doing nothing but growing since then. Also, she's really on edge because her husband rented a house in the Lower Garden District from none other than Glenda."

Veronica picked up another envelope. "Must be the one she bought from her mother."

"Glenda's *mother* owned a house in the Garden District? That cost serious money, even back in the day."

"Don't forget how popular burlesque dancers used to be. From the 1940's through the 1960's they ruled this town, some straight from the governor's office. Think Blaze Starr and Huey

Long. And you know burlesque still does a booming business here."

I did know that. There were several burlesque clubs, an annual festival, and even a school. "Her mom must've had a famous lover who bought her the place, because there's no way her Caressa the Crawdad Queen act earned that many clams."

She smiled. "Cute."

"You could even say whimsical." Take *that*, Baileys Mudslide Coffee Creamer. But the smirk fell from my face. The Mudslide reminded me of Glenda's ninety-year-old mother, a.k.a. Caressa the Crawdad Queen, mud-writhing in a barely there mudbug number, and the creamer curdled in my gut.

Veronica tossed the envelope in a basket she reserved for bills. "Why don't you take your friends to Friday Lunch at Galatoire's?"

"It takes social prominence and a line sitter to get a table, and I don't have either."

"The maître d' owes me a favor for a traffic warrant I helped him with, and I'm sure you could get David or Standish to wait in line—for the customary fee of twenty bucks a head."

I could take the girls for po-boy sandwiches for half that, but since David and The Vassal—as Standish was known—were college students who worked for us part-time, I didn't mind funneling them extra cash. Plus, Friday Lunch at Galatoire's was *the* New Orleans event, bigger than a Saints' game or backstage passes to Jazz Fest.

God knew Valentine, Kate, Merry, and I could use an event to make up for the disastrous bachelorette party last month. "Thanks, Veronica. I'll go ask the guys."

I returned to the lobby, relieved to find an empty reception desk. The Vassal was standing over the corner desk he shared with David, cutting a yard or so of brown faux fur that clashed with his blue-and-green plaid shirt. David was in his gamer chair studying a strip of Velcro-lined jute that he held across his chest like a sash.

8

I crossed my arms and leaned against the doorjamb. "Investigating a case for Miss Hunter America?"

David dropped the sash and held up long, skinny fingers that matched his lanky six-foot frame.

The Vassal gazed at me over the rims of his coke-bottle glasses. "Negative. We've been invited to walk with the Intergalactic Krewe of Chewbacchus, so we're fashioning our costumes."

The Sci-Fi-themed Mardi Gras krewe was infamous in New Orleans for its many pranks, so I was familiar with it. "In July?"

David flipped his longish bangs to one side. "We're required to make all our own throws. We thought we'd get our bandoliers done early."

"Seven months, to be exact. Out of curiosity, what's a bandolier?"

"Uh..." David swallowed and glanced at The Vassal, whose already slack jaw had lowered an inch. "Chewbacca's combination toolbelt and ammunition holder."

"Lightsabers use ammo?"

A hiss came from the back of The Vassal's throat, and David had fear in his eyes. The dorky duo gaped at me like I was an alien from Mars—or rather, their version of an alien from Mars—a human on Earth who'd never seen *Star Wars*.

The Vassal swallowed with his mouth open. "Wookiees don't use lightsabers. Their weapon of choice is a bowcaster."

David's head bobbed. "It's, like, a laser crossbow."

Someone ought to shoot them with a bowcaster and put them out of their nerd misery. "Speaking of 'Chew' and 'Bacchus,' I'd like to take some out-of-town friends to Friday Lunch, and I need one of you to stand in line. You know Galatoire's policy—no reservations since 1905, not even for celebrities and presidents."

They gazed at their Chewbacchus costumes.

"Vassal, with a name like Standish, you're perfect for the gig." I

9

pulled my wallet from my hobo bag. "Eighty bucks will make a lot of Mardi Gras throws...and furry sash thingies."

David popped up. "At your line-sitting service. But if we can't get a table, you should take your friends to Tales of the Cocktail."

"Not an option." I handed him four twenties. "One of them is pregnant."

The Vassal pushed up his glasses. "In that case, Postpartum Support International is having their annual convention this weekend."

My head gave a sad shake. These two were clueless to the ways of non-intergalactic females. "I've gotta run. Text me with the table info."

Gripping the strap of my handbag like a sling—a real-world weapon—I headed for the exit. As soon as I'd conquered Ruth and Glenda, the girls and I would have a good time no matter where we ended up for lunch. It was going to be great to have a nice, normal get-together after the Niagara Falls nightmare.

"Although," I hedged under my breath, "normal *is* a relative term in NOLA."

"NOT EVEN THE ANCIENT GREEKS—OR frat boys, for that matter— would live in these ruins." I slammed the door of my 1965 cherry-red Mustang convertible and surveyed the house that Glenda had rented to Kate and Jim.

Greek Revival mansions were common in New Orleans, but there was nothing revived about this one. It was a side hall double-galleried two-story with dingy gray paint and black shutters that were barely hanging on. And from what I could tell, the columns lining the front porch and balcony dated to the time of Aristotle. "The Acropolis is in better shape."

As I headed up the walkway to the front door, I heard voices coming from the backyard, a man and woman arguing. Great.

Got here just in time to hear Kate and Jim fighting about this dump.

Always one to eavesdrop, I tiptoed to the stone fence and peered through the wrought iron fleurs-de-lis adorning the top, as I was also one to spy.

A man in khakis and a white button-down was staring down a woman by a pool that might as well have been a swamp. He was in his mid-thirties, so he could've been Jim. But even though the female's back was to me, it was clear she was no Kate. The lady was ninety if she was a day, but her age wasn't what held my attention. It was the gray-blue dorsal fin on her back.

And the blowhole.

She stomped a sparkly blue kitten heel and waved an arm with a bat wing reminiscent of Ruth's turkey neck. With a well-rehearsed spin, she paced the length of the pool, shaking her bustle skirt and blue-sequined tail fluke. She stopped at the diving board and pointed a flipper mitten at the mansion.

The man scowled and moved his lips, but I couldn't make out any words.

The woman rolled her eyes, revealing a sparkly headpiece with a gray-blue beak.

It was odd that she'd dress as a dolphin in New Orleans. I mean, a gator or a crawdad, sure.

Wait.

A crawdad.

Like Glenda's mother's Caressa the Crawdad Queen act.

My hands went to my mouth. Oh, God. Did Glenda schedule some sort of pool show for her guests? "I'd better get inside and call off the skin reveal along with the skeezy rental."

I hustled to the porch, hoping the columns would hold a little longer, and pressed the doorbell. Instead of the standard ring, it played the famous jazz striptease number "The Stripper."

Kate opened the door in a blue sundress, looking tired and way more pregnant than I'd expected.

11

A beached whale popped into my head. It wasn't nice, but in my defense, she *was* wearing blue, and I'd just seen a dolphin.

Her eyes misted. "I'm so glad you're here, Franki."

I leaned over and gave her a hug. "Everything's going to be okay."

She wiped her tears. "I know. It's just that Jim and I didn't sleep a wink. Turns out, the master bedroom has a waterbed. I found that out when I sat on the mattress and fell in. And I didn't want to say this over the phone, but I'd swear there are ghosts in the attic."

"Why? What did you hear?"

"*Moaning.*"

Of course, I didn't believe in ghosts, but I wasn't surprised by the moaning. After all, this *was* Glenda's mansion. "Where's Jim now?"

"He's still so upset about the house that he went for a walk to cool down before you came. You missed him by five minutes."

Did I? Or was he the angry man out back with the displeased dolphin?

She gestured for me to enter. "Come into our humble abode."

I stepped into a red entryway that was more whorish than humble with zebra floor tiles and a stripper pole beside a narrow staircase that ran the length of the wall.

Kate pointed to gold curtains. "Behind curtain number one is a parlor, and down the hall is a kitchen and black dining room… with a table surrounded by bondage chairs."

"I'll take curtain number one." I parted the shimmery gold fabric and entered a hot-pink room furnished with a tiger rococo couch and cheetah and leopard armchairs. My eyes traveled up a leg lamp like the one from *A Christmas Story*, except that it didn't stop at the thigh.

Traumatized, my gaze shot to the pink satin fabric ceiling and landed on a chandelier with mating cherubs. "This place is as bad as the Park Avenue. The only thing missing is the body."

"It's worse than that hotel. I keep looking at pictures of my little Laurie to take away the sting." She pulled up a picture on her phone. "Here she is with Jim."

Still looked like a boy with that sparse mop, poor kid. But Jim was definitely the guy out back.

Kate lowered her phone. "I'm sorry. I don't mean to be rude about the house. It's not all bad. I like the red velvet pillows with the single pink blossoms."

"Those aren't blossoms."

Kate squinted at the pillows, and her eyes popped.

"Glenda took the color scheme from Madame Moiselle's on Bourbon Street, the strip club where she danced for decades. The idea is that it evokes the female body…intimately."

Kate sobbed.

I patted her back and led her to the couch. "The décor is definitely overstimulating—er, overwhelming. But, trust me, you get used to it."

She leaned against the questionable cushions. "I'm not so sure. It's quite an assault on the senses."

"I know." I sat beside her. "A terrorist assault."

Our eyes locked, and we burst out laughing. My "terrorist" reference had brought us both back to a crazy run-in we'd had with two FBI agents at Babette's bachelorette.

I wiped a laugh-induced tear from my eye. "Agents Summer and Winter are probably still somewhere in Niagara Falls, looking for that terrorist organization."

"If they aren't, we need them here to root out the terrorists who helped Glenda decorate this house. Want to see the bedroom?"

"No!" I yelled too forcefully. "It's time to get you out of this contract so we can meet Valentine and Merry for lunch and have some overdue fun together. By the way, what's Merry doing at the hair show? An ex-CIA agent turned Girl Scout Leader doesn't strike me as the fancy updo type."

Kate looked wistful as she smoothed her frizzy brown hair. "I'm not sure. Maybe Valentine wanted to tame those blonde curls."

"Well, as talented as she is, I'm sure she'll win, or whatever the objective of a hair show is. Speaking of winning," I rose from the couch, "I'm going to tell Glenda that the narrow staircase isn't sizable—I mean, suitable—for a woman in your condition."

"That's a perfect excuse!"

Fortunately, Kate hadn't caught my whale-sized slip of the tongue.

"While you call your landlady," she scooted to the edge of the couch, "I'm going to pop into the ladies' room, if you can call it that." She tried to shove off but rolled backward into the pornographic pillows.

"Let me give you a hand." I hoisted her up and pulled out my phone.

"Thanks." She rubbed her lower back. "That maneuver is getting more difficult."

Tell me about it. I discreetly massaged my bicep and followed her through the gold curtains. As she climbed the stairs, I decided to take a peek at the dungeon dining room. Besides being an eavesdropper and a spy, I was also a masochist—the figurative type, not the kind who'd use bondage chairs.

I dialed Glenda and walked to the end of the hallway, where there was a window overlooking the backyard. As the line rang, I peered outside to see whether Jim and the dolphin dame were still there.

I ended the call and texted David and The Vassal to get out of the Galatoire's line.

We weren't going to Friday Lunch.

And we weren't going to have fun.

Because the body I'd joked about earlier wasn't missing.

It was dead in the pool.

VALENTINE

ARLENE MCFARLANE

"Wow!" Merry sniffed the hairspray-filled air. "So *this* is what hair shows are like!"

We were at one of dozens of tables inside the huge ballroom at the New Orleans convention center, where I was attempting to do the impossible on Merry's curly blonde hair. Namely, attach an Ariel Barbie vertically to the back of her head.

First problem was Merry's hair lacked length. This made it tricky to hide Ariel's legs, considering the whole point of my creation was to braid Merry's hair around Ariel's body and produce a sweeping mermaid effect.

I conquered the short-hair dilemma by adding sparkly long turquoise extensions. But between Merry's constant squirming to admire the goings-on in the room, and me needing another set of hands to secure Ariel in place, it'd be a miracle to get the look right—all before the timer dinged. To be honest, I'd performed my share of miracles in the salon, but I was at a disadvantage here, only working with what I could haul to the show in my black beauty bag.

"My Girl Scouts would get a kick out of this event," Merry shouted over the din coming from blow dryers, music, and the amplified voices from the speakers on stage demonstrating the latest hair techniques.

I couldn't see the connection between hair shows and Girl Scouts, but I *mmmed* fittingly, then tuned out the commotion and finished braiding the turquoise extensions down her back. I left a few blonde curls kissing her cheeks and decided the tips I'd colored blue to replicate waves was a cute touch. After all, no first-rate beautician would miss an opportunity to enhance every last detail.

Plus, it couldn't hurt to wow the judges with something replicating a local flourish since New Orleans and burlesque water themes seemed to be a thing. Though I could've been way off. I didn't know a mer*maid* from a craw*dad*, but give me a lobster any day and I'd thermidor the heck out of it. I giggled inside. In truth, the wine mixed in a lobster thermidor sauce was the only way I could enjoy more than a teaspoon of alcohol without sliding to the floor plastered.

"Ha! Look at the updo on *that* woman. Marie Antoinette reincarnated." Merry wiggled her fingers through her crown, loosening what I'd just done.

I slapped her hand away. "Stop touching Ariel! Every time you move, it messes up her tail." Thank God I'd gotten the fluke at the end flared just right.

Merry shrugged good-naturedly. That was one of the things I loved about this woman. She was ex-CIA with all the traits of a special—and somewhat deadly—agent, and here she was volunteering to be my model at the L'Amour Hair Show...as I tugged and colored and lengthened her hair no less. *And* slapped her hand away to boot. Boy, was I saucy.

Romero was right. When I told him I was heading to New Orleans for a hair show a month after returning home from Niagara Falls, he threatened to tie me to my bedpost with his police handcuffs to keep me from getting into any more trouble.

While the handcuffs-to-the-bedpost sexy suggestion sent an

electric jolt to all points south, I promised him this trip would be different. I'd be in New Orleans for business, visit a few friends, and fly back to Boston in no time.

I was in the middle of restoring Ariel's frizzy red hair back to its original sheen when my cell phone on the table in front of Merry buzzed.

She waited a respectable beat, then rolled her gaze from my buzzing phone to my reflection in the mirror. "Are you going to answer that?"

"Nope."

"What if it's work? Or a family emergency?"

I grunted as I struggled with Ariel's wild mane. "For someone so carefree, you're awfully concerned about my buzzing phone."

She leaned back in her chair, a grin firmly in place, likely thinking about her Girl Scouts again. "I know from experience what happens when you ignore a call."

She was right. Normally, I'd jump on it. But the clock was ticking, and I was in the middle of a difficult job. Furthermore, if it were a family emergency, my mother would take the reins from God and handle everything.

If there were a catastrophe at work, Max, my righthand man, would pan things out. Plus, there was also Jock de Marco, the Argentinean Hercules in my salon who also happened to be an ex-navy hero. *He'd* come to the rescue. Jock had a calming effect on everyone he touched.

Gulp. Nix that. His sexy touch was anything *but* calming. Something I worked to overlook.

"Valentine!" Merry pulled me back to the moment, signaling to my phone dancing in circles on the table under her nose.

"Oh all right!"

I wiped my hands down my corseted white jumpsuit, my flared pant legs swooshing as I pounced forward and picked up the phone before it fell off the edge of the table. I said hello, then did some head nodding, took a sharp intake of air, and finished with a thick swallow.

"What is it?" Merry's eyes widened with expectancy.

I lowered my arm in slow motion and drew my mouth down at the corners—a typically unflattering look. But now wasn't the time to fret over appearances.

"That was Franki. She just witnessed a dead body floating in a swimming pool at the Greek Revival mansion where Kate's staying. The police are there now. They're arresting Jim for the woman's murder."

"Jim? As in Kate's husband?"

"Sounds like it. From what I could make out, Franki said the woman was dressed like a glitzy dolphin, but I couldn't hear everything over the noise in this place." I snatched my beauty bag from under the table and dumped all my tools inside. "We have to go."

Merry's gaze slid up to her widow's peak. "What about my hair? And the contest? Isn't this going to be judged?"

"Would've been, yes. But it can't be helped." I looked from her hair to the busy ballroom. "Nobody'll even notice we're gone." I wouldn't bet on this. When I'd registered for the hair show, I'd been asked to speak on a panel regarding the latest tips on makeovers. I was depended upon, and it crushed me inside not to live up to my commitment. But I couldn't reveal that to Merry or let Franki and Kate down.

"Okay." Merry shrugged. "So I walk around with an Ariel doll sticking out of my crown. I'd once led a presidential motorcade dressed as the Statue of Liberty. Of course, that gold-painted torch in my right hand was actually a submachine gun that, come to think of it, felt as comfortable in that costume as this mermaid feels on my head."

I hitched my bag over my shoulder and gave Merry a wink. "You'll live."

"Yeah, but I have a feeling today's fancy-shmancy New

Orleans lunch is out."

WE HOPPED out of the Uber minutes later in front of a creepy old mansion—the kind horror shows were made of. The coroner had just pulled away, and the police dragged Jim in handcuffs to a cruiser. Kate was at the curb calling out to Jim not to worry, and Franki was next to her, jabbing her pointer finger into a plainclothes detective's chest like he was a pin cushion.

"You have no right arresting an innocent man." Franki's tone was confident, her manner unyielding.

"Listen, Amato," the handsome, middle-aged detective's voice was rooted in exasperation, "keep your PI nose out of this. You think the NOPD doesn't have anything better to do than pick on innocent people?"

"Basically, yes."

"Ha. Ha. If this week's visiting dignitary wasn't such an egocentric jerk, we'd have more men to put on this case."

"All the more reason for *us* to come to the rescue." Merry bounced onto the curb alongside Franki.

"Who's this?" The detective shifted his gaze from Franki to Merry in her turquoise tankini top and oceanic-looking, satin, ruffled bell-bottoms.

"My friend, Merry Wrath." Franki did a once-over at Merry in her getup, deliberately choosing not to address the ABBA throwback outfit. "She's ex-CIA, if you must know."

"Now Girl Scout leader." Merry smiled, giving a dismissive wave. "But that's a story for another day."

The detective raised a suspicious eyebrow. "You know you've got a doll sticking out of your head?"

Her smile widened. "Another story. For another day."

He rolled his stare to me.

I had one arm around Kate, trying to comfort her while

19

simultaneously trying to keep my skin from crawling from the mansion and its crumbling stone-and-wrought-iron fence.

"And that's Valentine Beaumont." Franki gestured, palm up, to me.

I batted my thick eyelashes and waved my fingers at the detective, my sparkly bracelet and ring glittering in the sunlight.

He assessed me from the top of my straightened burgundy hair down to my frosted lips and corseted white jumpsuit, to the tips of my buckled spikes. "Who are you supposed to be? Kim Kardashian's double?"

I smirked inside at the reference. Truth was, Kim and I did share the same Armenian background. And it was better than being pegged, as I often was, as *that impulsive hairstylist who'd made a soprano out of a killer by clamping a perm rod around his family jewels.*

"She's a beautician," Franki boasted, "who could teach *you* a thing or two on charm *and* who has the problem-solving skills to craft extraordinary defenses with her beauty tools."

He brightened, evidently impressed. "Like MacGyver?"

I patted my beauty bag and gave him my specialized impish smile—which I saved for toads like this...and, well, Romero, when I was trying to get away with something.

He stepped off the curb and backed up to his cruiser. "Y'all have my blessing. Your friend will be held in Central Lockup until we have time to process this case. You find any evidence that proves him innocent, let me know."

"We will," Kate said through a sniffle, "Detective..."

"Mangiaratti." And with that he angled into his black-and-white and screeched away from the curb.

"Rat eater," Franki muttered.

"*Franki!*" Kate blinked in shock though it looked as if she were concealing a grin.

"*What?* That's the meaning of his name in Italian."

Merry spread her arms wide, attempting to get everyone to focus. "Well…now what?"

"Now we solve this case." Did I just say that? Oh boy. Romero was going to have a big macho conniption if he knew I'd uttered those words *or* became involved in another homicide case.

"Absolutely." Kate made fists, her knuckles white from the strain. "I'm not about to let Jim rot in a stinky New Orleans jail. Although, maybe it's nicer than *this* place…" She peeked up at Franki. "No offense."

Franki gave an indifferent nod. "You've got the stinky jail part right."

"Uh, excuse us."

We were so wrapped up in the moment, no one noticed two elderly men hobbling toward us, both wearing dark suits and long faces.

The talker was stocky at 5'8" and had a deliberate bow-legged gait. He had scruffy white hair, scruffy eyebrows that seemed in a constant state of frowning, and a suit jacket that looked like it hadn't been pressed since Eisenhower ran for office. He nodded sadly to the huge house behind us. "Did something happen to Caressa?"

"Sorry?" I stepped away from our circle to face the men. "You are…?"

"Boudreaux. Buddy for short." His face fell another few inches. "Caressa's a friend of ours." He thumbed the air over his shoulder. "Tibs and I live down the street."

Kate peered from Buddy, her expression motherly, to the other man. "You're Tibs?"

The second guy was the same height as Buddy but appeared shorter on account of his bald head. "If you must know, sweetheart, it's Thibodeaux. But that might be too many syllables to pronounce for someone in your condition."

Kate gasped at the sarcastic remark, too shocked to speak.

"Caressa doesn't live here anymore," Franki said, "so why

don't you two gentlemen move along? It's a hot day, and there are lots of watering holes on the next corner."

"What are you, hard of hearing? Buddy asked a question. We see a police car roll away, and he starts to worry, rubbing his hair into a bird's nest. Can't you see the guy's concerned?"

Tibs was right about the bird's nest. Any other time, me, a comb, and a razor could work magic on Buddy.

"You kids, you know nothin' 'bout what it's like to be old. Has-beens." Tibs went tight-lipped. "Everyone ignores you. We used to be a hot commodity back in the day. Spent our nights guarding Caressa and the other dancers."

I looked at my surroundings. "As in burlesque dancers?"

"Yeah," Buddy piped.

I hoisted my bag up my shoulder though the sweltering heat continually made it slide back down. "You were actual bouncers?"

"Don't look so surprised." Tibs crooked a sparse eyebrow at me. "We carried a lot of weight. No one got to Caressa without our say-so, or Arthur's."

"Arthur?" I looked up and down the street, expecting a third elderly gentleman to appear.

"Arthur's still in the biz."

Right. Like I was supposed to understand how someone older than Moses was still bouncing in a bar. Best not to picture it, I told myself.

"That dame had one of the best acts in town," Tibs went on. "Caressa the Crawdad Queen was her stage name. She could writhe in the mud like nobody's business."

He came back to the present, tugged on his jacket, and gave a sideways glance up at Franki. "Hey, PI, why don't you make yourself happy. Go handcuff someone."

Franki blinked open-mouthed down at Tibs, then narrowed her eyes. "How'd you know I'm a—"

"I *do hear* things, you know. I'm not dead *yet*."

He turned from Franki to Merry. "You know you got a mermaid attached to your head?"

Merry grinned. "Yes. Don't you love it?"

"Yeah, sure." He rolled his eyes, turned to me, and did a bats-in-the-belfry motion with his finger to the temple. "Her parents ignore her as a kid?"

Buddy reached an arthritic hand to his pal's arm. "Come on, Tibs. Times have changed. No one wants to tell us anything."

Tibs jabbed his hands on his waist. "We're not leaving till we know what happened to Caressa."

"Caressa hasn't lived here for a while," Franki explained, "not since her daughter, Glenda, bought the house from her."

Buddy's frown deepened. "Then who did we see the coroner take away?"

Kate pursed her lips as if she were about to explode. "We don't know, okay? The woman was murdered, and the cops are blaming my husband, Jim."

KATE

DIANA ORGAIN

J tuned out the chatter from the grumpy old men, cradled my head, and tried to think. This trip—that was supposed to be a fantastic surprise and getaway with Jim— had taken a turn for the worse. Not only was the Garden District home a joke, but what? Now the police had taken Jim to Central Lockup. On top of everything else, the only thing I could focus on was how hungry I was.

Weren't we supposed to get lunch?

Jim wouldn't mind if we grabbed a quick bite. I mean, how was I supposed to think if I didn't eat something soon?

And these twins! They were having a rip-roaring rock-'em-sock-'em battle in my belly. I knew they were starving. The power bar I'd had on the cab ride over had barely taken the edge off. I looked up to see Franki frowning at me.

"Kate," she whispered confidentially and out of earshot from Buddy and Tibs. "I saw Jim arguing with that lady."

"What?" Jim didn't argue with strangers.

Franki grimaced. "I didn't want to say anything in front of Detective Rat Eater, but Jim and that woman, she was dressed as a dolphin—"

24

Buddy's head popped up. "A dolphin, did you say?" Spittle flew out of his mouth in Franki's direction.

Franki stepped away from him and looked offended, her cat-eyes narrowing. "Watch where you're slinging that saliva, *sir*."

Buddy ignored her order. "A dolphin! Could it have been Delphine?"

"That's ridiculous," Tibs exclaimed. "What would Delphine be doing here?"

"Who's Delphine?" Valentine asked.

Buddy moved around Tibs to answer Valentine. I couldn't make out what he said. I only saw that he and Tibs both clasped their hands above their heads and raced toward each other bobbing up and down as if they were re-enacting a dolphin show of some sort. They whooped, hollered, and screeched.

Inside my belly, it felt like the twins were doing the same dolphin routine as Buddy and Tibs. I gripped my middle and rubbed frantically trying to soothe their agitation.

While Valentine and Merry politely watched Buddy and Tibs, I pulled on Franki's elbow and ushered her away from the screaming duo. "Do you think we can grab lunch?"

Franki's shoulder stiffened, and her eyes grew wide. "You want to eat *now*?"

My jaw tightened. "It's not a matter of want. I *have* to eat. I'm so hungry I can't even tell you. Where can we get a hamburger around here?" I glanced around the courtyard praying golden arches would appear.

Merry crossed over to us, the mermaid in her hair jiggling as she walked. "Don't worry, Kate. Among the four of us, we're going to figure out how to get Jim out of Central Lockup STAT."

"She's hungry," Franki said.

Merry quirked an eyebrow. "Oh. Well, now that you mention it...it *is* lunchtime."

I fanned my face. "And it's so hot here. Maybe we can get some iced tea or lemonade."

"It *is* roasting," Merry agreed. "I could go for a Sazerac."

Franki held her hands up in the universal STOP language. "Guys, as much as it pains me and my stomach to say this, we can't just go grab lunch and cocktails. We have to call an attorney for Jim."

"They're going to release him," I said. "They have no grounds to hold him. I know he'll want me to feed the twins."

Poor Jim. Part of me felt terrible prioritizing food over my darling husband, but the *hangry* part of me insisted on calories for survival, not to mention a brain boost for clarity.

"Kate, this is New Orleans! You're assuming the police need a reason to hold him. They don't. They need a reason to release him. And we have to give them that reason. They're not going to investigate on their own."

From across the swamplike pool, Valentine called out. "Hey ladies, what do you think that is?" She pointed to the filthy water. Peeking between a clump of algae and a partially deflated flamingo-floatie, a hollow iridescent casing bobbed up and down.

Merry made a face. "Garbage."

Valentine crossed to the corner of the courtyard and grabbed a pool net. "It looks odd. Out of place."

"So...hamburger?" I pleaded with Franki.

"Hamburger?" Buddy's eyes bulged. "Mama! You're in New Orleans. I forbid you to get a hamburger!"

"Gumbo, crawfish étouffée..." Tibs said.

My mouth watered.

"Jambalaya or New Orleans Muffaletta..." Buddy said.

My tummy rumbled.

"Po-boy or red beans and rice," Tibs called out.

Merry licked her lips. "Yeah..."

"And for dessert, beignets or bananas Foster," Buddy said.

"Or New Orleans Pralines or bread pudding," Tibs said.

I turned to Franki. "He had me at gumbo."

Franki nodded. "I get that you're hungry."

"Hungry?" Merry repeated. "The woman is pregnant with twins."

"Twins?" Buddy said. "That's nice."

"Did you ever see *Alien*?" Merry said. "She's got two of those things in there!"

I nodded. "Sure feels like that."

"If we don't feed her soon, those two are going to pop out and they're going to be *angry*!" Merry said.

"Very angry," I agreed.

"We absolutely have to feed the pregnant woman!" Merry declared. "Believe me. I work with children, and no one wants to get between them and a meal. Those suckers will bite your head or hand off sooner than look at you!" Then she leaned in conspiratorially—almost poking my eye out with the mermaid stuck in her hair. "If you want to start with dessert, you'll get no argument from me."

I shook my head. "I want to eat everything they just rattled off. Gumbo, crawfish, jambalaya—"

Merry nodded. "Got it. Two of everything."

Franki dug her cell phone out of a pocket. "First, I'm calling Louis Armstrong."

"What?" Tibs demanded.

"*What a wonderful world!*" Buddy sang, fanning his arms out and holding the last note. He ended with jazz hands.

Tibs applauded.

"Not that Louis," Franki said. "Kid I know. Attorney. For Jim."

"That's a great idea. Thank you, Franki." I wiped the sweat from the back of my neck and pulled at the top of my sundress to fan my face. "Seriously, how hot is it going to get?"

Buddy and Tibs chuckled.

"Oh, mama. We're not even close to the high for today," Buddy said.

"We should get her a parasol," Tibs said. "Doesn't Glenda have one in her fancy house?" He jabbed a thumb in the direction of my seedy rental.

"I didn't see a parasol in there," I admitted. Although I wasn't willing to say out loud that I was actually afraid to look.

Valentine, who'd been quietly poking at the items in the pool, snagged the floating half orb in the water and pulled it out with the net. "Look at this. What do you think it is?"

"Looks like a prop," Tibs said.

"You think everything's a prop," Buddy retorted.

"Hello, Louis?" Franki said into her phone. "Got a little situation here."

"Is he free for lunch?" I asked. "Tell him we'll buy. We'll tell him everything over a hot bowl of gumbo."

Merry gave me an enthusiastic thumbs-up.

Buddy pulled the plastic half globe from the pool net and turned it over in his beefy hands. "It does kind of look like a prop. Like what? An oyster?"

Tibs elbowed him out of the way and snatched the item. "It looks like part of a soccer ball. Maybe from one of the kids across the way. Little devils. Always up to no good."

"It's not that," Merry said. "Trust me. But it *is* half of something. See this ridge around the edge? It looks like it snaps into something else. Like a plastic Easter egg."

Valentine pushed the algae around the pool with the net, and another piece to our puzzle surfaced.

"That's it!" Buddy shouted, grabbing the net out of her hands.

"Um, hello?" Valentine blinked at Buddy in surprise.

From across the courtyard, I could hear bits of Franki's conversation with the attorney. "Central Lockup...yeah... Mangiaratti...said they got a visiting dignitary in town...I know...no one is going to work this case...wants to eat!" On that last note she chanced a look at me, then looked away when I caught her eye.

She thinks I'm crazy.

28

Guilt—for not pulling out all the stops for Jim—fluttered through my belly, quickly replaced by a hungry pain of epic proportions.

Wait a minute! There's no reason for me to feel guilty. I'm carrying twins!

Inside the pocket of my sundress my mobile phone buzzed. I pulled it out and saw an incoming call from *unknown.*

"Answer it," Merry said, catching me screening the call.

"Probably spam." I shrugged.

"Probably Central Lockup," she said.

Shoot!

I fumbled to grab the call before it went to voicemail, jabbing the green circle and giving a tentative "Hello?"

"Kate!" Jim's voice filled the line. "Don't panic, okay, babe? But this is my one call."

"I'm not panicking. I'm hungry."

Jim chuckled. "In that case, I might be happy to be here rather than with you."

I laughed with him. He knew all about the ravenous hunger I fought while carrying two new little lives around. "I'm so sorry you're in there, honey. Really, I am. But do you know what kind of food they have in this town?"

"Yeah. Sure. That's one of the reasons we came."

"Exactly. But instead of sitting in a fancy place stuffing my gob, I'm roasting in the hundred-degree heat, watching a few good ole' boys re-enact a dolphin burlesque show, while Valentine and Merry pull evidence out of the swamp!"

"Wait. Evidence? What swamp?" Jim's voice filled with hope.

"I mean, the filthy pool."

"Uh. Yeah. It is a pretty gnarly pool. Sorry about that. The Airbnb had old photos. Anyway, what evidence?"

"It's probably nothing." I watched Merry snap together the two halves of the item Valentine had retrieved from the pool. "Valentine found an Easter egg thing."

"Oh." Jim sounded deflated. "Listen, Kate. The cops here aren't like in San Francisco. The place is jam-packed with inmates, and it almost felt like they were going to forget about me, but then Detective Maserati—"

"Mangiaratti," I corrected.

"What?"

I bit my lip to suppress a laugh.

What was wrong with me? Jim was in some hellhole, and here I was giggling.

"Never mind, sorry," I said, trying to be more supportive.

"Anyway, Maserati said they found something in my things, but I have no idea what he's talking about. Told me to call a lawyer."

"Already on it," I said.

"Really?" His voice was hopeful.

"Absolutely! Franki's got a guy. We're having lunch, and I'll tell him everything. Then you and I will be on track for a romantic dinner tonight, okay, honey? Don't worry about a thing."

Franki hung up at the same time I did, and we turned to face each other.

"Jim needs a lawyer," I blurted, suddenly grateful to Franki for being so practical.

She nodded. "Louis is on his way."

Merry snapped to attention. "I'll meet him out front."

Franki squinted at Buddy and Tibs, tossing the lightweight item to each other. "What's that?"

"A sunken treasure," Valentine said with a smile.

MERRY

LESLIE LANGTRY

It was very hard to be taken seriously when you were dressed in a turquoise tankini, with ruffly satin bell-bottoms that mimic the undulating ocean waves, and a mermaid doll braided into the back of your hair. Now that I thought of it, there was that night in Bangkok with former British PM Boris Johnson (who, you might be surprised to know, has the same pants).

This was a bad situation, and I'm not referring to my bizarre attire. Kate's husband had been arrested for murdering an old… and I mean, *old*…burlesque dancer whose act involved dolphins… or she was a dolphin…or something like that. Valentine and I were at a loss, because New Orleans wasn't our turf. Franki had this in hand…we hoped.

Kate looked miserable, and I wasn't sure how to help. Of course, I'd been around dead bodies before, but none of those experiences prepared me for a dead burlesque dolphin chick in a friend's rented swimming pool. No wait…there was that time in Estonia with the dead Finnish spy dressed as a chicken, floating in the kiddie pool at Angela Merkel's niece's baby shower. That's kind of the same thing.

31

"I'm sure everything will be fine," I'd said to Kate a few minutes ago with no real evidence that it was true. "I'll grab Louis and then we'll go to lunch."

"Thanks, Merry," Kate had said, rubbing her back. "I thought this was going to be a nice romantic vacation, not one where Jim would be charged with murder."

I was now sitting on the front porch, waiting for the lawyer. I hoped he was a good one. I hoped Kate could hold on a little longer. And I hoped wherever we went they'd have frosé wine slushies—something I'd heard was popular here and expected to experience at least once. Or twice.

My cell buzzed, and I pulled it out of a pocket in my satin pants. It was a text message from home.

First off, the text from Lauren, one of my eleven-year-old scouts, said, *Nobody died. And that's good news, right?*

Why did these things always happen when I wasn't home? *Explain*, was all I texted back.

A well-dressed couple in their sixties strolled by and froze when they saw me.

"I'm a mermaid!" I said brightly before they started scurrying away. "It's not that weird!" I called out after them. "Not for New Orleans!"

It's not bad. Okay, so Mr. Ferguson...your husband, Lauren felt it important to remind me of my relationship to Rex, *asked us to house-sit for a couple of hours because Betty has started a pet-sitting business that's going to be a front for something she calls money laundering. Are you supposed to wash your money? Because I've never seen my parents do that.*

It was as if time had stopped. My husband did what? Rex was the town detective, and, I thought, smarter than this.

Do I still have a house? I had to ask because last time they burned down my garage.

Your house is fine! It's just that...um...we...I'll send you a picture.

An image appeared on my cell. I screamed. Philby, my obese

cat who looks like Hitler, used to have white-and-black fur. Now it was electric orange. And she didn't look happy about that.

You guys do not want to make the cat angry, I typed quickly before directing them to where the canned tuna was. *Set it down in front of her and back away slowly, without making eye contact!*

Hopefully they didn't do this to the other animals, which included Martini—a narcoleptic cat, Leonard the deerhound, or Rufus the golden poison dart frog. Huh. How would you dye a frog? Maybe Valentine would know.

Hey guys! It's okay! We now appeared to be on a text loop as this came from Inez. *Mrs. Wrath doesn't know about the other thing!*

I responded immediately. *The other thing?*

How did you know about that? There was a pause between Ava's replies. *Hey guys, she knows about the other thing now! I think she's psychic!*

I'm not psychic, I typed quickly. *You literally texted me about it. What is the other thing?*

She asked about the other thing again! one of my four Kaitlyn M's texted. Another one finished the other's thought—which I always suspected meant they operated with one hive mind. *What do we do?*

I can see all of your texts, I responded.

Hang up! came a text from Inez.

Still here, I insisted. *And I'm pretty sure you can't hang up a text stream.*

She can manipulate time and space! a text from all four Kaitlyns' cells declared at once.

What happened? I was losing my patience.

Betty's cell said, *This never happened. Goodbye.*

I stared at my phone, wondering if Valentine also knew how to un-dye an angry, electric orange cat, when a car pulled up. The driver looked too young to be a lawyer and too Caucasian to be Louis Armstrong. The kid got out of the car and waved. If he thought it was strange that I had multi-

33

colored hair wrapped around a mermaid doll, and was dressed like an aquatic-themed drag queen, he didn't say anything.

"Hi!" he said, still standing next to his car. "Ms. Amato called. I'm the lawyer."

"*You're* Louis Armstrong?" I blurted.

He nodded. "I know, I know, I'm much taller. That throws people off."

"No, it's not that..." My mind raced for a way to explain my outburst without sounding stupid.

"Is it the mustache?" He pointed to what appeared to be three, single hairs beneath his nose.

Me and my mermaid doll shook our heads.

Armstrong looked confused for a moment before snapping his fingers. "It's the accordion! That threw you off!"

I was just about to tell him to forget it when he pulled an accordion from the backseat of his car and began playing and singing "When The Saints Go Marching In."

I stood up and walked down the steps to him. "You're right. That's it. I didn't see it before. Come on, I'll take you to Franki, and then we'll go feed the pregnant woman. By the way, where do they serve frosé around here?"

Louis seemed disappointed as he threw his accordion back into the car and slammed the door. He took two steps toward me before a young, stunningly beautiful woman hesitantly approached us. She had glossy black hair that cascaded down her shoulders, and curves that would cause a fifty-car pileup in any third-world city.

"Excuse me," she said. "I'm looking for Delphine?" As she drew closer, her eyes went up to my hair.

"How do you know Delphine?" I asked warily. That was the dead dolphin chick, right?

"I'm Concepción." She held out a perfectly manicured hand. "I'm Delphine's granddaughter."

I shook her hand and wondered how to tell her that her grandmother's body had just been taken away.

"Is she here?" She looked uncomfortable. "I need to see her before she does something bad."

Louis, who seemed immune to her charms, shook his head. "You shouldn't say anything that may implicate you in a crime." He pointed to himself. "I'm a lawyer. I know these things."

Concepción's eyes grew wide. "I knew it! She didn't mean to do it! It's…" She seemed to search for the right words. "Dementia! She can't help herself."

I held up my hands to stop her. "Help herself from doing what, exactly?"

Concepción bit her full, red bottom lip. "My *abuelita* said there was something here she needed. She said it should've belonged to her. I swear, Delphine wasn't in her right mind when she called to tell me she was coming over to steal it."

"Your grandmother…" I started, "Delphine…came here to steal something by accident?"

Louis turned to me. "This woman needs representation. You can't badger her like this." He looked at Concepción. "Don't worry. You can't charge a dead lady for a crime."

The woman froze. "What did you say?"

I shoved Louis away so he couldn't do more damage. "I'm sorry." I patted her arm. "I'm afraid I have some bad news about your grandmother."

I told Concepción what had happened, leaving out that the cops thought it was murder or that they had a suspect in custody. The last thing I needed was this woman freaking out on Kate.

"Dead?" The color drained from her face. "No, that can't be right. She just called me. You must have the wrong dolphin."

Concepción had dug in her heels and refused to budge as I tried to lead her. I needed to get these two to the others so we could clear this up and feed Kate.

"Come on. My friends are around back. We'll get this sorted."

I cast my I'm-going-to-disembowel-you-with-a-can-opener look to Louis "The Accordion" Armstrong so he'd keep his mouth shut.

It didn't work.

"I can represent you, too." He pulled a card from his wallet and handed it to her.

"Um, no, you can't," I said. "We really need to find the others."

"Of course I can." Louis snatched the card back. "I'm a *lawyer*. And if you can't get compensation from the murderer, we can file a civil suit."

"Murder?" Concepción's large brown eyes grew larger.

"That's enough, Louis," I growled. "We don't know that it was murder."

The kid ignored my anger. "Of course it was! Old strippers don't just die. They *always* get murdered. This is New Orleans."

"She wasn't a stripper!" Concepción screamed. "She was a burlesque dancer!"

The others probably heard that. I grabbed each of them by an arm and dragged them around the house.

"We don't know anything yet," I snapped at Louis. "I'm taking you to Franki, *now*."

Franki, Valentine, and Kate must have heard us because they looked at me curiously when we rounded the corner.

"Oh, hi, Ms. Amato!" Louis grinned when he saw her.

Valentine sized the lawyer up and down. "*This* is the attorney for Jim?"

"Who's Jim?" Delphine's granddaughter asked.

"My husband." Kate wobbled a bit unsteadily.

Concepción started piecing it together. "Your husband murdered my *abuelita*?"

My friends turned their eyes to me, and I shrugged.

"This is Delphine's granddaughter, Concepción. Surprise!"

FRANKI

TRACI ANDRIGHETTI

"How did your Jim kill my *abuelita*?" the Salma Hayek lookalike shouted, gaping from the pool back to Kate. "Did he strangle her? Slam her head on the pool deck?" She gave a dramatic flip of her black mane and bared her teeth. "Or did he hold her head underwater until her lungs filled?"

My hand went to my chest. For a grieving granddaughter, she was graphic.

Kate held out her hands. "You need to calm down, Concepción."

The woman stomped a strappy red sandal that matched her lipstick. "I'm not one of your brood, *madrecita*, so don't tell me what I need to do. What happened here?"

"Don't call me *madrecita*." Kate stomped *her* swollen foot, and then rubbed it. "I have no idea what happened to your grandmother, but I know my Jim didn't lay a finger on her."

"Did he lay something else on her to knock her unconscious?" Concepción shrieked.

The footwork escalated to flamenco-dance level, but my eyes were on the pool. Was there a weapon in the water? The police

37

hadn't checked, and I almost couldn't blame them. That green-brown sludge was teeming with bacteria.

Merry sidled up to me. "Funny thing happened out front. Concepción told Louis and me that Delphine called her in the grip of dementia and said she was coming here to steal something that belonged to her."

Louis straightened in his oversized suit. "That's hearsay."

Merry blinked. "Right. I heard Concepción say it."

I scanned the back of the mansion for signs of a break-in, like a broken window or hole in the screen door, but everything appeared intact. "That must be why Jim was arguing with Delphine. He caught her trying to enter or exit the house."

Louis laid a prosecutorial look on me. "That's supposition."

"Whose side are you on, Armstrong?" I asked, getting in his baby face.

Merry shot me a side-eye. "He's representing Jim *and* Concepción."

"Well, well, well." My tone oozed contempt. "I didn't know your mom raised you to be an ambulance chaser."

Louis jerked his suit coat and looked over his shoulder, probably for his hovering helicopter mother. "She raised me to be an attorney and an accordion player."

"An *accordion*!" I half laughed. "Is she Italian?"

"Sicilian, to be exact."

No wonder the woman was all up in his business.

The stomping ceased, and Kate rushed to Louis. "I overheard you mention your mother. By any chance, did she pack you a lunch? Like some of that thick Sicilian pizza?"

He leaped back, shaking more than his head in his too-big suit. Honestly, I related to the kid. Kate looked as innocent as Little Red Riding Hood, but the Big Bad Wolf was in her eyes—and he was eating for three.

I seized on the ceasefire to question Concepción. "I'm a PI. Would you mind telling me what Delphine came here to get?"

Her haughty gaze flickered over me. "Uh…she didn't say."

From the way she'd hesitated, I didn't believe her. "Where did she call you from?"

"The Burgundy Bar."

Valentine adjusted her corseted jumpsuit and rose from the table by the pool, where she'd been observing the scene with Buddy and Tibs. "Maybe we should pay a visit to the bar. You know the place, Franki?"

"It's at the Saint Hotel. They're known for burlesque, and it's the same décor as inside the house."

She blinked at the mansion, beautifully defined eyebrows raised at the gaudy exterior. "How would you label the inside?"

I smirked. "Bordello chic."

Concepción's lips curled. "Or brothel chic, in this case. According to my *abuelita*, Caressa is nothing but a lowlife Jezebel harlot."

Tibs rubbed his bald head. "Old Caressa does get around."

"How?" I huffed, incredulous. "The woman moves at the pace of an actual crawdad." Realizing I might've offended Buddy and Tibs, who were no spring chickens, I added, "Which makes her act super convincing."

"Ha!" Concepción threw her head back. "Caressa's nothing if not an actress. For all we know, *she* murdered my *abuelita*."

I put a hand on her forearm. "Trust me on this; if Caressa had killed your grandmother, she'd still be making her escape from the pool to the gate."

She yanked away from my touch. "I'm not leaving until I find out what happened. Someone needs to check the pool for a weapon."

"Be my guest." I gestured to the pool. "But FYI, the water itself is a weapon. Actually, multiple weapons. Cholera, dysentery, typhoid fever."

Buddy grinned and clasped his hands across his belly. "I'd like to see what Merry the Mermaid Girl can do in the pool."

The comment verged on creepy, but I agreed. Merry did have a water theme going with that outfit and hairdo.

"I'm game," Merry said, hands on her hips, "as long as someone has a wetsuit."

Valentine retrieved the pool toy from the table now that Buddy and Tibs had finished playing catch with it. "I don't think that's necessary. This round plastic ball, or whatever it is, is most likely the weapon."

Concepción spun on Kate. "I'll bet your husband cracked it over her head. She was old and frail. Hitting her with *anything* would've killed her."

Merry shrugged. "It *is* split in two."

Kate's eyes grew as big as the plastic ball. "Whose side are you on, Merry?"

"Just an observation," she said, hands raised. "I'm Switzerland, unlike Louis Armstrong here."

"Hey-y-y," he whined. "I can sue you for slander."

"Try it," I growled, "and you'll be the one dredging the pool."

He leaped back. "I can't get wet. I'm being treated for keratosis pilaris."

Alarmed, I leaped back, too. "What's that?"

"Blocked hair follicles," Valentine volunteered. "The common name is chicken skin."

Kate pulled me aside. "Speaking of chicken, there must be a Popeye's nearby. I read that the franchise started here in New Orleans."

We had to get her some food, and soon. Otherwise, there'd be another murder—one of us, when she wolfed us down. I was about to propose we break for lunch, but sunlight glinted off the pool toy, and I took a closer look. It was round—as Valentine had pointed out—not egg-shaped, and it looked familiar. I scratched my temple. Something wasn't right, starting with a burlesque dolphin act.

"Excuse me for a few minutes." I pulled my phone from my

jeans pocket and walked toward the house for privacy. I texted Glenda the lowlights of the day and told her to get to the mansion. Next, I called David and The Vassal's cell phones, but neither answered. Odd, because they should've been back at work.

Reluctantly, I dialed the office.

"Private Chicks," Ruth rasped.

"It's me. Can you pass me to David or The Vassal?"

"Nope. They went to an art supply store for stuff to make bandolier blocks, the slackers."

A buzzer blasted into the receiver and knocked my hearing from one ear out the other. When I recovered, I gritted my teeth. "Why'd you *buzz* me?"

"You're a bad influence, that's why. The boys told me you paid them to stand in line at Galatoire's while you're out gallivanting with your girlfriends. Now they're blowing the money you gave them on the art supplies."

When I found the ChewbacchanALIENS, they were going to get a chewing out, and then I was going to beat them with those bandolier blocks. "If you see them," I said, teeth still clenched, "tell them I need info on Delphine the Dolphin Girl, and whether she had a connection to Glenda's mother, Caressa the Crawdad Queen."

"I can tell you that."

"Great." I waited.

Silence ensued, followed by ice clinking in a glass, the pop of a pull tab on a soda can, and a long, slurpy sip.

My grip on the phone tightened. "Are you going to tell me?"

"Now that you've asked."

A tension headache threatened to erupt. If Delphine had even half the attitude of Ruth, then I could almost understand why someone had killed her.

Ruth chewed a piece of ice to amp up my agony. "Delphine

41

and Caressa had a notorious feud. One night they had it out on Bourbon Street."

"A cat fight, eh?"

"No, a crawdad and dolphin fight."

Fair enough. "What about?"

"You sure are pushy, missy. You can get the information yourself." She slammed down the receiver.

One of these days, that turkey-necked ostrich and I would have it out. And when I was done with her, the only thing left would be her cat-eye glasses.

Shoving my phone into my pocket, I crossed the lawn. Valentine and Merry were consoling Kate under the shade of a magnolia tree, and Concepción was on the phone, pacing the yard. I went to Tibs and Buddy's table and took a seat. "What can you gentlemen tell me about a feud between Delphine and Caressa?"

Buddy rubbed his thighs. "Aw, they had a big blowout at the 500 Club on Bourbon Street. It was owned by Leon Prima, the brother of the famous jazz musician, Louis Prima. You know him?"

Before I could answer, he launched into the chorus of Prima's big hit "Pennies from Heaven."

I'd investigated a homicide connected to the theft of one of Prima's trumpets and the true story of the Axeman of New Orleans, but I limited my reply to a nod. "Do you think the feud had anything to do with this mansion and how Caressa paid for it?"

"If you're implying that Caressa stole money from Delphine, she didn't need to. Burlesque was big business in the 40's and 50's. Those girls had their own hairstylists, maids, assistants, agents, and managers."

Tibs nodded. "Some even got on magazine covers and had parts in movies, like Blaze Starr and Lilly Christine the Cat Girl."

I half smiled. "I'll bet Lilly got into some cat fights."

"Why would you think that?" he snapped.

I sighed. Unlike his friend, the guy had zero sense of humor. "Let's go back to Delphine and Caressa. What started the feud?"

He narrowed his eyes on me, unfriendly like. "Delphine used a kiddie pool in her act. She'd chitter and flop around—"

"Like dolphins," I interrupted. Again, no laughs.

"…and strip off her costume," Tibs finished. "One night when a Hollywood agent was in the audience, Caressa filled the pool with live crawdads. Delphine came out to a packed house and got in the water."

Buddy chuckled. "It's pretty hard to look sexy or land a movie deal when you're getting pinched by dozens of crawdads."

"True dat," Tibs said. "Once Delphine plucked off the crawdads, a brouhaha broke out bigger than the time Kitty West, God rest her soul, took an ax to Divena's water tank on stage at the Casino Royale."

I'd heard that story somewhere before. "Didn't Kitty have a stage name?"

Buddy bobbed his head. "Evangeline the Oyster Girl."

"That's it!" I smacked the table. "The pearl!"

"Sure." Tibs grunted. "Oysters have pearls."

"No, I mean, yes, but that's not what I mean." I looked at the girls, who'd gathered around the table, in time to see Valentine lean into Merry. "Has Franki been drinking?"

Merry's head tilted. "I hear New Orleanians start as soon as the bars open."

Kate stared into the distance, rubbing her belly. "She hasn't been drinking. When we were talking earlier, her breath smelled like coffee…and beignets."

We really had to get Kate something to eat. "What I'm trying to say is, the oyster reminded me that Glenda once said Caressa originally wanted to be Pearl the Clamshell Girl."

Tibs eyed me as though I were the one who'd been cracked over the head. "So what?"

I flattened my hands on the table, bracing myself for what I was about to reveal. "The pool toy is not an egg or a ball. It's a pearl. And the last place I saw it was on Caressa's clamshell bed in the house where she currently lives."

"HOLY CANNOLI!" Kate raised her head from the magnolia tree where we'd gathered to wait for Glenda.

Was she still obsessing over Louis's mother's Sicilian food? I sat up and followed her gaze to the gate, where my landlady was entering in a familiar red-and-black flamenco-stripper outfit. "Oh, Glenda's getup. If anything, it's holy guacamole."

"Castanets as pasties?" Valentine arched her brow. "Oy vey."

I rose to my feet. "I said the same thing the last time I saw her wearing it, and she informed me that it was an *olé*."

Merry, who was lying on her back, raised onto her forearms and bent her knees, sending her ruffled pants swooshing. "I see Glenda's skirt ruffle, just not the skirt."

"Yeah." I brushed grass from my clothes. "You'd think she left that in Barcelona with the rest of the costume, but no."

"Barcelona." Kate swallowed. "I'll bet she ate a lot of tapas."

I shook my head. "As far as anyone knows, Glenda survives off cigarettes and champagne."

Valentine giggled. "She'd better be careful. Smoke is hard on platinum hair." She patted her beauty bag. "I have blue shampoo that would keep it from discoloring and drying out."

I glanced toward the mansion, where Concepción and Louis were having a client-attorney meeting in the parlor. "I'd better head off Glenda before the grieving granddaughter comes out and takes offense at her outfit."

As I crossed the yard, Glenda flashed a wan smile. "Where's the crime scene, Miss Franki?"

It was tempting to say *You're wearing it*. But I went with, "At the pool." I steered her toward the water. "I'm surprised you wore your flamenco costume. Concepción *is* Spanish."

Glenda fondled the long fringe that hung from her choker. "That's why I wore it, sugar. Out of respect."

Showing up half naked—make that four-fifths-naked—when someone had died wasn't respectful, unless she was trying to rouse the dead for a wake. "Respect for whom?"

"A Spanish dignitary is visiting the city, and when you texted that Concepción was here, I assumed he was with her."

"Why would you think that?"

"Her mother is the product of Delphine's affair with the dignitary, the former King of Spain's cousin, and he's in town for the annual Running of the Bulls."

The affair didn't surprise me given what Buddy and Tibs had said about the heyday of burlesque, but I was surprised about the king's cousin's travel plans. "Then someone ought to tell the guy he should've stayed home, because the Running of the Bulls is in Pamplona."

"We have it here, too, sugar. And afterward, the king's cousin is the honorary guest at La Fiesta de Pantalones."

I wasn't sure how NOLA pulled off a bull running, but one thing I *was* sure of—Merry belonged at that Pants Party.

"Miss Glenda!" Buddy waved. "How's ya mom'n'em?"

She sashayed to the table. "Where y'at, fellas?"

Surprised by the intimate local greetings, I looked at my landlady. "Do you know Buddy and Tibs?"

She touched the silk rose in her hair. "They're long-time fans, naturally."

My gaze dropped on the men like a gavel. "After following her mother's career, you follow hers, too?"

Buddy elbowed his friend. "We're diehard supporters, ain't we, Thibodeaux?"

Tibs's lips slid into something akin to a grin. "Keepin' it in the family."

Bumps rose on my arms—of the goose variety, not, thankfully, like Louis's chicken skin. Something about Buddy and Tibs wasn't quite right, and they were hanging around after Delphine's death, which was just plain wrong. Most people couldn't wait to leave a crime scene to avoid being implicated. The fact that the two men hadn't left had landed them on my suspect list.

Glenda sashayed in six-inch flamenco-stripper heels to the pool's edge, lit her signature Mae West cigarette holder, and blew out the smoke. "It's just sad, sugar."

"Of course it is. Someone died."

"I was talking about her shoes." She pointed to a blue heel the police had left behind. "Kitten mules on a dolphin is way off the mark."

Yeah, a couple of animals off.

She huffed out a puff. "I mean, you can't seduce a man in heels that low, which is one of the reasons her career never took off like my mother's. But I have to give old Delphine credit. The Dolphin Girl was a clever act."

"How so?" I remained baffled by the concept.

"Child, it drove the Flipperophiles wild."

Flipperophiles? That was a thing?

She ashed her cigarette in the pool. "Did you check the water for a weapon?"

"No, because that sludge is lethal. If you're going to rent this place again, you need a pool boy."

"I have one, sugar, but I keep him busy at the fourplex."

We didn't have a pool at the fourplex, but I knew better than to ask about his duties. "Valentine did find what I think is the pearl from your mother's bed. It was in two pieces in the pool."

"Strange." She took a drag. "I distinctly remember putting it on the master bed."

My head swam like the bacteria in the pool water. Delphine probably found the pearl when she'd entered the mansion, but that news didn't bode well for Jim. "Are you positive you didn't put it down somewhere and forget about it? Like the backyard?"

"I didn't go into the backyard. I borrowed a few tchotchkes from my mother's place to finalize the décor before the guests arrived, but mum's the word, Miss Franki. She doesn't know I took her pearl."

"Then why'd you take it?"

"It's perfect for the deep-diving theme in the boudoir. I'll show you."

She strutted to the house, and I followed even though I wasn't looking forward to going back inside, or to her interpretation of deep-diving in a bedroom.

We entered the back door. As we strode the length of the hall and up the stairs, I uttered a silent prayer that Concepción and Louis would stay in the parlor. When it came to feisty, the foot-stomping Spaniard had nothing on Glenda, who was dressed and ready for a flamenco fight-off.

Glenda clomped up the long, narrow stairwell, and as I climbed after her, I was careful to check my footing. Halfway up the steps, I spotted a blue sequin that matched the ones on Delphine's tail fluke.

The Dolphin Girl *had* been in the mansion.

Glenda arrived at the second-floor landing and entered the first room on the right.

Hurrying to catch up, I held my breath before walking into the deep-diving room. If *The Little Mermaid* had ended with Ariel ditching the prince and going into the brothel business with Ursula, it would've looked like this.

In the middle of the ocean-blue boudoir was Glenda's mother's signature piece of furniture—a clamshell waterbed with a mirrored interior. Presiding over the clamshell was an anatomically correct, life-sized statue of Neptune with his trident.

Glenda pointed to two decorative pillows on the bed. "I put

the pearl right there, Miss Franki, between the sexy mermaid and the randy seahorse."

Good thing she'd split those two up. "Kate didn't see the pearl or she would've said something." I wandered around the bed but didn't notice anything unusual, except for the bed itself. "Although, she did say she fell into the mattress."

Glenda chewed the tip of her cigarette holder. "Is she the pregnant one?"

"Twins."

She batted her false lashes. "That explains it, sugar. She caused a tidal wave that knocked the pearl between the bed and the wall."

The theory was plausible. Kate and the kids would've made a sizeable splash. "Delphine probably came up here and stole it while Kate and I were in the parlor. By the way, what's the back-story on that pearl?"

"You'll have to ask my mother, but right now she's doing a show."

The clock was ticking for Jim, so we needed to speak to Caressa soon. "What time does she get off?"

"Oh, it's an all-day performance."

Probably because the woman moved so slow. "Where at?"

"An all-you-can-eat crawdad boil at the Burgundy Bar."

Where Delphine had been when she'd called Concepción. Kate would finally get lunch—if she had the stomach to eat while watching a scantily clad ninety-year-old woman writhe in mud.

VALENTINE

ARLENE MCFARLANE

$\mathcal{W}$e were not "passing a good time," as New Orleanians liked to say. Delphine had swum her last lap—so to speak, Kate's husband was stuck in some dingy jail for her murder, Concepción had shown up, throwing accusations as to who killed her grandmother, and if we didn't go to the Burgundy Bar soon where there'd be food, I was afraid Kate would slurp the slimy algae from the pool.

I dug into my beauty bag, suddenly remembering I had a packet of ginger snaps from the flight that I hadn't eaten. Maybe that would satisfy Kate until we found some real sustenance. I pulled out the cookies when Max called on my cell.

"Tell me again why you fled to New Orleans and left me at the salon with the dimwit of the century?"

The dimwit Max was referring to was Phyllis Murdoch. Next to Jock—the superhero in our salon—Phyllis was my third employee. While I didn't approve of Max's incessant taunting of her, there was some truth in his statement. Phyllis had about as much skill at her job as the Sphynx cat had hair. A smarter boss would've fired her long ago, and I'd tried. But Phyllis was like an ingrown toenail. She always came back.

49

My chest tightened, and the sense of impending doom filled my bones. I'd left Max in charge for a few days. He wouldn't be calling if it weren't important.

"You know I came here for the L'Amour Hair Show." I took an anxious breath and moved away from the others. "What'd she do now? And you better not tell me there was another explosion in the shop." One a decade was enough.

"No explosion, but there must be a reason she's dressed like a French maid today."

Why'd this come as a surprise? Phyllis was the Coco Chanel of badly made clothes: every week a new theme. "Maybe she got a job cleaning houses."

"*Ha!* Phyllis can't even clean her station. Who'd hire her to clean their house? Anyway, never mind her." Max could hop from one topic to the next without batting an eye. "Did your fancy hairdo win?"

I peeked over my shoulder at Merry who was rotating her head in circles, giving Ariel the ride of her life. "Uh...not exactly."

"What?" he screeched. "Do I need to fly down there and set the judges straight? You're the most talented stylist I know. How could you not have won?"

I smiled inside at Max's devotion, choosing to overlook the times he'd thrown me under the bus—even if it had been for my own good. "I was sort of called away from the hair show."

"Uh-oh." Max paused. "I know what that means. Who dropped dead?"

"Nobody you know, okay? The woman was ninety-some-thing, dressed as a dolphin, and was found floating in a pool."

"Why was she dressed as a dolphin?"

It was a reasonable question. "She was a burlesque dancer, and that was part of her getup." Sounded bizarre even to my ears.

"So...you're at an old-age home for burlesque dancers."

"Not exactly. And I have to go. Can this wait until I get back?"

"Sure it can wait. I'd *love* for it to wait."

Brother. Trust Max to pique my interest. "All right, already! What happened at work?"

I could almost see the frisky grin spread across his face. "Remember the time you and Jock were locked downstairs in the laundry room?"

"Yes." My cheeks tingled at the memory of being pinned between Jock's hard-muscled body and a damn vibrating washing machine.

"And remember how you got that lock fixed?"

"Max! What happened?"

"The dimwit got herself locked inside the laundry room."

"So let her out."

"I'm debating."

"About what?" Max could be infuriating.

"About the wisdom of doing just that. Nobody's asking for her," he reasoned. "Jock and I are handling the clients, and Phyllis took half a pizza downstairs with her to eat while folding towels. When you think about it, she's probably happy as a pig in mud, having her own picnic while evading work."

He had a point.

"You still have to let her out, okay? I'm on my way to the Burgundy Bar. I don't have time for this."

"The *Burgundy Bar*!" Second screech of the day.

I jumped from his shriek and clasped a hand to my chest, exhaling a breath. This was what I had to put up with in an employee? I waited a beat until my pulse returned to normal. "You know the place?"

"Lovey, before I came to work for you, I *did* have a life. I used to Mardi Gras it up and enjoy the odd burlesque scene. The Burgundy Bar on Canal Street was *the* place to go, and I mean, it was beyond lively. Everything has a devilish appeal and is decorated in a deep shade of red. The walls, the curtains, the lighting from the bar. Even the chandeliers glow red." I heard a gratifying

51

sigh through the phone. "Once you go there you may never come out."

And I'd suggested going there to my friends? What had I been thinking? I was tempted to ask if Max wanted to switch places with me, but if we were going to find answers on how Delphine ended up dead in a pool at a house that once belonged to her rival, then I had to put my sleuthing cap on and start sleuthing.

"If you need my help," he continued, "I'm but a phone call away."

Max's idea of *help* was never being there when I needed him. Case in point, when Jock and I'd been locked in the laundry room. Any other time, Max had his ear to the wall. When I needed him most, he became Mr. Invisible.

"Thanks. I'll remember that." I said goodbye, disconnected, and tossed Kate the cookies.

THE FOUR OF us piled into Franki's cherry-red Mustang convertible and headed for the Burgundy Bar. The breeze felt good on my face, and I finally had a moment to appreciate my surroundings. We passed one beautifully restored mansion after the next until Franki took a sharp right turn. Kate and the cookie she was munching on almost landed in my lap, and Merry's Ariel headpiece dropped sideways, giving the appearance of an arrow skewered through her hair.

"Woo-hoo!" Merry shouted from the passenger seat, arms high in the air. "I love convertibles! Reminds me of the time I drove a jeep in reverse in Turkmenistan farm country." She wheeled around in her seat to look at Kate and me. "You don't want to know the outcome of that ride. But I will say I didn't know pigs could actually fly."

"I'm glad you're on *our* side," Kate said, wiping crumbs off her chest.

I nodded in agreement, but I was really focused on Merry's hair. I had to fix Sideways Ariel, if only for my own peace of mind.

"I should probably tell you guys…" Franki glanced at Merry, then eyed Kate and me in the rearview mirror. "Concepción's mother is Delphine's daughter whom she had with the former King of Spain's cousin. According to Glenda, this is the dignitary who's in town, and he's here for the annual Running of the Bulls."

I reached forward, nudged Merry to turn her head to the front, and straightened Ariel so she was upright again. "I thought the Running of the Bulls took place in Spain."

"Evidently we have it here, too." Franki cocked an eyebrow high, then gave a slight shrug. "Don't know how I missed *that* newsworthy event."

"Ooh…" Merry rubbed her palms back and forth, the friction adding to the sweltering heat, "now *that* sounds like fun."

"Wow." Kate gobbled the last piece of ginger snap and dusted off her hands. "I'd love to run with the bulls."

We all slid her a funny stare.

"I mean," she elaborated, "not now, obviously. Just in general, you know?"

I gave her an affirmative wink. "Spoken like a true mother. And hey"—I settled back in my seat—"what was Concepción's exit all about? One minute she claimed she wouldn't leave until she found out what happened to her grandmother, and the next she pulled a disappearing act."

"Maybe she was sick of listening to Louis Armstrong," Merry offered.

"Maybe," I agreed. "Then again, maybe she's hiding something."

We all chewed on that, two minutes later pulling up to the curb in front of the Saint Hotel.

"I'll park," Franki said. "Meanwhile, you guys go in and see what you can learn. We need answers! Plus, see if you can find

Caressa. The woman's so damn slow, it shouldn't be hard to spot her."

I slung my bag over my shoulder and followed Merry and Kate into the hotel. The blast of A/C was welcome, made better by the smell of smoked sausage, lemon pepper seasoning, and dried dill.

Once my eyes adjusted to the crowded, dim interior of the Burgundy Bar, I could see what Max was talking about. The atmosphere was lively, the horns, saxophone, and drumbeat saucy and loud. Everything was a deep shade of red. Except the floors. They were checkered black and white.

Kate scurried to the buffet for the all-you-can-eat crawdad boil, and Merry and I stood gaping from her departure to the stooped woman all but fossilized on stage.

Merry poked me, her voice loud over the hoots and hollers. "Glenda's mom?"

I blinked three times, afraid my eyes were playing tricks on me. But the woman moving in slow motion in a skimpy crawdad getup was no joke. I snapped my mouth shut. "Afraid so."

Caressa struggled to flip a boa over her shoulder, and if her tap dance routine slowed another beat the staff could tip her into an upright coffin. "Suddenly I have visions of Shirley Temple tapping to 'On the Good Ship Lollipop.'"

Merry's own Shirley Temple curls bounced through her loosening hairdo as she searched the room. "Didn't the poster outside say something about her act being in the mud?"

"True dat," I said, borrowing from the locals. "Maybe she didn't want to ruin her crawdad outfit or her corncob-heeled shoes."

Merry squinted at Caressa's heels. "Or the crawdad on each toe. Maybe the mud act comes later."

The audience hooted at Caressa to show more skin, albeit leathery and saggy. She raised her bony arm, the loose skin under her bicep flapping as she waved away their hoots.

"I'd like to see what comes off next," Merry said, "but I've got to hit the little Girl Scouts' room."

I gave her a questioning glance.

"*You know.*" She jerked her head toward the ladies' room. "Nature calls."

"Got it," I shouted over the noise. "Go ahead."

Merry took off, Ariel swinging to and fro at the back of her head. This prompted a smile on my face. Gosh, she was a good sport, walking around in public in that sea-world outfit. She could give Phyllis and her French maid costume a run for her money.

Well? I was here for a purpose. Not that I was eager about poking around a burlesque bar, asking questions concerning Caressa or Delphine, but the sooner I got to it the sooner we could leave.

I shook the nervousness from my hands, inhaled a gulp of air, and waded through the crowd, picking up bits of conversations about the women. Failing to glean much, I asked the odd drinker if they'd seen Delphine in the bar today.

I got a few shrugs, several dirty looks, and one proposal, and I hadn't even gotten to the part about Caressa's past sabotaging act on Delphine. Most eyes were glued on Caressa who suddenly stopped her routine, set her two rickety feet apart, and bent over, coughing and gasping for air.

Cough. Cough. Wheeze. Gasp.

Everyone in the room froze, the seconds ticking by, the same question likely on everyone's minds. Was this going to be Caressa's last performance?

Good grief. I needed to find out what that historic fight with Delphine was all about—and fast! What if it had something to do with her murder? I didn't think there was physically any way that Caressa could've done her in, but what if there was a link?

Franki had mentioned there was friction between the two women that resulted in a war of wits. But there had to be more to their animosity toward each other than one filling the other's tank with nipping crawdads.

Caressa straightened to her former stooped position, tugged out a set of false teeth, and picked off what looked like a crawdad's shell. Seemingly the culprit of the coughing fit, she flung the shell into the audience, reinserted her dentures, and took her final stiff bow.

"Caressa, wait!" I called out in a hoarse whisper before she made her exit.

The seasoned burlesquer cranked her head over her shoulder at me, then clamped an arthritic hand on her neck as if the action almost did her in. Without giving me another glance, she hunched forward and shuffled off the stage as if on her way to soak in a tub of Absorbine Jr.

I was about to tiptoe around the stage to catch up with Caressa when a gruff old stagehand in a white shirt and saggy tan pants grabbed me by the arm, tacked a mound of pink feathers on my rear, and gave me a shove to the platform. "Go on. You're late!"

"Late?" I sputtered through loose feathers floating in the air, staring from the rope tattoo on his wrist up into his eyes. "Sorry. You've mistaken me for some—"

"You're in a corset, aren't you?"

I gaped down at my jumpsuit. "Yes, but I'm not a—"

"No buts!" He tugged my bag off my shoulder and pushed me past the curtain. "You signed up for this, so no complai—"

He stopped short and eyed me suspiciously. "Wait...a... minute. You're that broad I saw disturbing the audience a few minutes ago. What are you trying to do, ruin the act?"

"*No.* I...uh...I'm a reporter." I was almost ashamed to admit that the line came easily. "I'm doing a story on the early years of the famous Caressa the Crawdad Queen. She's a legend in her own time. Er, truly someone to aspire to," I added, laying it on a bit thick.

"Reporter, eh?" He gave me a wizened eye, absently tucking my bag under his arm.

"Uh, yes. And you are...?" What the hell. If I was going to fake this career I might as well make the most of it.

"Arthur's the name. Stagehand's my game."

Arthur. Arthur. Where had I heard that name before? I examined the deeply etched lines around his eyes and mouth, guessing him to be around eighty, when it hit me. Buddy and Tibs had told me earlier that Arthur was still in the biz. He wasn't exactly a bouncer as he might've once been, but as a stagehand he seemed to be doing a bang-up job.

"What do you want to know about Caressa?"

I gazed down at my trusty bag nestled next to his armpit. If I wanted it back I'd have to say something, yet I didn't want to tell this buffoon that Delphine had been murdered. "It's common knowledge that there was bad blood between Caressa and Delphine the Dolphin Girl. Do you know what caused their dissension?"

"Ha, do I *know*? You don't go around the block as many times as me to not learn a thing or two."

The crowd was growing listless, and the catcalls and groans grew louder.

"Look," the guy said, "I'll tell you a secret about the women if you go out there and do a number."

"But I'm not a dancer." I peeked over my shoulder as the lights flashed and the sassy music fired up. The audience gave a loud whoop of anticipation. After Caressa hobbled off they seemed eager for live bait.

I organized my thoughts, turned back to Arthur, and let out a heavy sigh. "*Fine.*"

Sheesh. How did I get in these messes?

He leaned in and gave a satisfied wink. "Delphine was involved with a Spanish dignitary, the king's cousin, Eduardo... something, something de Borbón."

Hmm. So we have a name. "Yes, I'm familiar with that story." And the fact that Delphine had had a baby from the tryst.

"Aha, but did you know that she'd stolen Eduardo from Caressa?"

"What?" Did Franki's landlady know this about her mother? "What happened?"

"Eduardo and Caressa were in love and were planning to marry until Delphine put on the charm and broke it up. After that, Caressa was never the same. I was a young whippersnapper at the time, but one night when I went to tell her she was due onstage, I found her in her dressing room, flat out on her couch, makeup smeared, crying into a bottle of bourbon."

He shook his head, remembering the scene. "The room was a disaster. Broken pictures. Smashed bottles of brandy. Booze dripping down the walls. And Caressa shouting obscenities at Delphine, who was nowhere in sight. She was so plastered we had to cancel her act. And she wasn't much better the next night or the next. I was afraid when she came out of her alcoholic-induced haze she'd kill Delphine. Got to the point no one wanted to be in the same room when those two females came face to face."

"How sad." My voice was so low I barely recognized it.

He shoved me toward the stage. "What's even sadder is what'll happen if someone doesn't get out there before the crowd erupts. And you did promise…"

"All right, all right. Don't get pushy."

"Come on!" someone hollered from their seat. "Show us what you got!"

I plodded onto center stage with a weak smile. What *did I* have? "A-choo!"

This elicited a few giggles from the audience. Right. I glanced over my shoulder. I had feathers. At least they were pink.

I squinted at the throng through the glaring lights and tapped

58

my toes to the music, buying time, my mind still on the shocking news of Caressa's crushing past.

"Booooo!"

Oh boy, this wasn't going well. And where the heck was the stagehand? A tip or two would've been nice. He finally poked his head past the curtain and gave me an eye roll.

"Show us some skin!" someone yelled.

I took an anxious breath, flipped my hair off my shoulders, and waved my arms around like the Village People signing Y-M-C-A. Only I was signing H-E-L-P.

There were some jeers, and one person hit me in the boob with a wedge of pungent cheese. "'Cause your act stinks!"

Sweat trickled between my shoulder blades, and my heart was thumping like a jackhammer. I looked up in silent prayer. *Save me, Lord, from this circus act.*

I made sweeping circles on the stage and tripped over the sagging feathers. *Shoot!* Where were my pals? Wait. Was that Franki in the back corner? Who was she talking to? I blinked. Detective Mangiaratti? What was he doing here when he already told us the police didn't have time to deal with this case?

Darn.

I tried to signal Kate, but she was sitting at a table wearing one of those big lobster bibs, cracking crawdad tails and sucking the heads.

I pranced around onstage, doing a can-can here and a shoulder shimmy there. My legs had taken all the kicking they could muster, and my nerves were shot. Where was Merry, and how long did it take to hit the little Girl Scouts' room?

Aha! I spied her at the sideline deep in conversation with a lady by a kiddie pool. The woman seemed to be forcing a gold piece of material with colorful gems onto Merry.

"*Psst.*" Arthur tossed me my blow dryer and whispered loud enough for my ears only. "I don't know what a reporter's doing with a blow dryer, but it's your only hope!"

He plugged it into an extension cord and nodded at me. I gaped back at him, open-mouthed, but he motioned to get on with it, and then turned his back. Wonderful. Now all I needed was someone's hair to style.

I absently swung the blow dryer around and around by its cord in a large circle, thinking this through.

Everyone hooted and whistled. Things were looking up.

Confidence boosted, I flicked on the blow dryer and aimed it at my face, then up and down my torso. My hair blew back in cascading waves, and the feathers on my rear swayed in the breeze. I sashayed across the stage, getting the hang of things.

I toyed with the eyelets at my breasts, popping one, two, three. Then I bent over, slid the blow dryer back to the side, and gave a sexy twist toward the audience, picturing Romero as my sole spectator.

Adrenaline surged through me, my mouth suddenly dry at the thought of stripping for the man of my dreams. If I wanted to get through this act and get to Caressa, I was willing to give it my all.

"Take it off!" someone yelled.

Hold on a sec. That voice! My hands froze on my eyelets, and I scrutinized the crowd.

Buddy? Tibs? What were *they* doing here?

I'd heard Romero say time and again that killers often hung around a murder scene after snuffing someone out, or they weaseled into an investigation. Was that true? Were Buddy and Tibs involved in Delphine's murder? Following us in hopes of learning something?

I was trying to piece together the conversations back at the house and found I'd lost my place on stage. I stood there, attempting to retrace my steps. Didn't matter. The drinking crowd had had enough of my talent.

"Bring on the next act!" someone yelled.

"Yeah," another one howled. "This one dances like Caressa!"

Being compared to a ninety-year-old woman wasn't doing a

lot for my ego. "That suits me *fine!*" I shouted to no one in particular.

I marched off the stage, stuffed my blow dryer back in my bag, and looked up in time to see Arthur unravel a hiding Kate from behind the curtain and push her into my recently vacated spot.

Huh? I didn't know how our expectant mother of twins made it up here or when she'd changed, but she was swathed in a gorgeous green satin dress, tummy out a mile wide, and she was clenching the restaurant's bib in her hand, a crawdad still stuck to it.

KATE

DIANA ORGAIN

o Do

1. Get Jim out of jail.
2. Solve Delphine's murder. (Is it really a murder?)
3. Feed the twins.
4. Ride a steamboat.
5. Take the haunted ghost, voodoo, and vampire tour.

I took center stage and motioned to the hot bright lights above. I prayed there was actually a sound crew behind the hot lights and that they'd been told my music selection. I held my hand high and said at the top of my lungs, "Here she is, boys!" I waited anxiously for the music.

On cue, the tech crew played "Rose's Turn" from *Gypsy*.

Relief swept through my body as I swung my hand dramatically down, pitched my hip to the left—albeit almost toppling over—and sang the next line, impromptu-style. "Here I am, world! Here's Kate!" I flung both my hands in the air and paused.

The crowd cheered as the music bellowed. This had been an audition song for me back in the day. I knew it by heart. I hadn't really wanted to take the stage, but Valentine's poor act had been a disaster, and the staff had threatened not to serve me any more mudbugs unless I got on stage.

That would teach me to murmur, "Even pregnant with twins I could do better."

Recently, I'd visited with my college drama buddy, Babette, and apparently by the eagerness I'd taken the stage, I was feeling nostalgic about it.

Now I felt ridiculous, pregnant and prancing around onstage in front of a drunk crowd.

What would Jim say? *"Kate, okay, you had to eat, I get it. But did you have to get onstage?"*

All these thoughts rushed through my head, and the lyrics to "Rose's Turn" flew out of my mind. Fortunately, I was good at improv. Even though I sang, "Blah, blah, blah, blah," the crowd went wild, cheering, "Take it off, mama!"

Okay, that was it. Time to take a bow and exit stage left.

The raunchy jeers, paired with the fact that it'd been too long since I'd used the restroom, fueled me to speed up the finale. I channeled my inner Liza Minnelli, arched my back, and punched at the sky.

The crowd erupted in more lecherous taunts as my back protested and I teetered forward.

Good gracious!

I spotted Franki, Merry, and Valentine in the crowd. They were grinning madly and cheering along with everyone.

"Help me!" I mouthed to them, but the crowd only cheered louder.

Forget it.

If there was anything you learned as a new mom and budding PI, it was that there were some situations only you could get yourself out of. I took a quick bow, put a hand on my aching back, and wobbled as quickly as I could off stage.

Thankfully away from the lights, I immediately accosted the stagehand. "Restroom, stat!"

He nodded and wagged his gnarly finger toward the dressing room where I'd changed. Great. I'd ditch my costume and get some relief.

Once inside the gaudy dressing room, I panned it for the restroom. "Excuse me," I said to a woman in her fifties, fussing with the longest lashes I'd ever seen. "Where's the powder room?"

The woman looked me up and down, snarling at my belly. "You know, you can get a size down on those faux bellies. They're cuter."

I refrained from pulling off her faux lashes and scratching out her eyes along with them. "I'll remember that. Now, the ladies' room?"

She gestured to a red shower curtain in the middle of the room.

I squinted at her. "What?"

She nodded knowingly. "Ah. You're new here." She flung the curtain back to reveal a grungy, dirty toilet.

I gasped.

The woman laughed. Other ladies, peering at themselves under bright makeup lights, giggled at me.

Before I could respond, the tiniest man in the world, or close to it, sauntered in with a large bucket of fried chicken. The dancers descended on him like a pack of hungry wolves.

Goodness!

I thought *I'd* been starving. This was worse than a shark feeding frenzy. The man disappeared under the bucket and the women, and I feared for his life.

I took advantage of the chicken distraction to step out of the green satin costume and slip back into my comfy maternity sundress.

Just then, Concepción entered the room, chatting angrily on her cell phone. "It's gone!" she said. "Now what do we do?" Without looking where she was going, she slammed into the circle of women scarfing down the chicken. She gasped, horrified. When she spotted me, she ended her call abruptly and sauntered over.

From the depths of my pocket, my phone buzzed. I dug around for the phone and slipped it into my hand. Next to me, Concepción pouted when she saw I was prioritizing a call over her. She propped herself on a nearby stool.

I spied Vicente's handsome face on the screen. He was video-calling me. I swear that man had a sixth sense.

Did he know I was in a room with half-naked women?

I accepted the call and panned the room for him.

He broke out in a grin. "I knew I should've gone with you and Jim to New Orleans!"

"No," I said. "This trip's a disaster. Jim's in jail, I just danced on stage in a strip club, and it's hotter than Hades here."

He laughed. "I heard about Jim. That's why I'm calling."

I narrowed my eyes. "What? How did you hear about Jim?"

"Your mom called me."

"What? How does Mom know about Jim?"

"He called her."

"No. I was his one call."

Vicente's charming smile filled the screen. "Well, he, you know, talked to the police and told him you were pregnant with twins and feared this news would put you into early labor, so they let him call your mother."

Next to me, Concepción edged herself into the screen of my phone.

Vicente's eyes widened. "Oh. Maybe I need to fly out there after all."

Concepción giggled. "Who's your friend, *madrecita*?"

"It's *Kate*!" I clapped a hand over the screen. "And he's a PI in

San Francisco *and* a terrible womanizer. You don't want any part of him."

Concepción blinked her dark lashes at me. "No?"

Vicente cleared his throat. "I think I can get a red-eye tonight."

"Ah. That's a Spanish accent!" Concepción said, a flirtatious lilt in her voice.

"*Sí!*" Vicente said, eagerly.

"You need to visit us here in NOLA," Concepción said.

"No, no, no, Vicente. You don't need to come," I said. "I have this under control. My friends and I are perfectly capable of getting Jim out of jail."

Concepción stiffened as if suddenly remembering that my husband was the prime suspect in her granny's death.

"Vicente," Concepción said, "Kate and her so-called PI friends couldn't get a dog out of a pound. If her husband is guilty, I hope he rots in jail."

"Jim didn't kill your grandmother!" I said. "I can literally guarantee you. The man wouldn't hurt a fly. This is all a horrible misunderstanding."

Concepción glowered, then tears sprang to her eyes. "*Ah! Mi abuelita!*"

"Don't worry, *guapa*," Vicente said. "I'll take the red-eye and get to the bottom of what happened to your *abuelita*."

MERRY

LESLIE LANGTRY

*F*or the sake of honesty, I'd admit that I've wrestled in mud before. The first time was in Colombia, when I was with Carlos the Armadillo. I'd had two options, wrestle Paco the Pantless in mud, or wrestle Ophelia the Octopus in a pool filled with uncut heroin. I chose Paco. There was a reason Ophelia was known as the Octopus and it wasn't pretty, due to her two extra arms and the weird way she seemed to change color when she'd had a snootful of heroin.

The second time was when I was undercover with the Yakuza in Okinawa, where, for the amusement of my boss, I had to wrestle a female sumo wrestler named Pippy in a hot mud bath. That one didn't go as well as the fight with Paco because Pippy was a trained wrestler and Paco was a nitwit who thought the Three Stooges had *sick moves*.

The last time may not technically count. I was in actual mud on the ground, fighting for my life against a rival strongman who'd criticized the strongman I was with. It was kind of an honor thing there, and I'd drawn the short straw to defend Azlan. I won by the skin of my teeth, which is good because the loser

67

had to wrestle my guy's pet grizzly. You probably didn't need me to tell you that the grizzly won.

At least I had the right apparel in my previous encounters.

"You want me to wrestle in *this*?" I held up the one-piece outfit that looked like a swimsuit, covered in gold sequins studded with fake jewels, with hot purple feather trim that made it look like my breasts had sprouted angry eyebrows and my thighs had a flamboyant Muppet beard.

"Owner has a dry-cleaning business," the woman rasped as she took what appeared to be a difficult breath. "Look, I just work here. I don't make the rules. This is what you gotta wear."

Caressa the Crawdad was making her way, slower than the definition of *slow*, to the kiddie pool filled with mud. Halfway across the room, she froze and looked around curiously. After someone ran over and whispered in her ear, an expression of realization came across her wizened features and she started her molasses-like walk in our direction.

"But she's got to be pushing ninety!" I protested. "I can't wrestle someone that old! What if I accidentally kill her?"

The woman shrugged. "You got five minutes." She spared a glance at Caressa. "You'd probably be safe with ten." And then she walked away.

Valentine strode over and leaned in, whispering, "See what you can get out of Caressa. All I got was that she and Delphine were bitter rivals because Delphine stole the former king's cousin from Caressa." She stepped back. "Good luck!"

Right. This was for Kate. Time to do my bit. I handed Valentine the mermaid doll and looked at the mud and the outfit. "Where do I change?"

FIVE MINUTES LATER, I was in my end of the kiddie pool, and Caressa was about twenty feet closer but still not in the pool. Two bouncers picked her up, carried her the rest of the way, and set her in the mud. After a few minutes of adjusting her outfit, she slowly froze into a high school wrestling stance.

I didn't want to hurt her and I wasn't kidding when I'd expressed my fear of accidentally killing the old woman. I'd definitely have to bring my D game for this, especially since I'd also have to interrogate her during the event.

Men were standing around the kiddie pool, leering and carrying on as if this were Stripper Fest. I'd seen most of them egging on Valentine and Kate earlier. You could practically taste the stench of misogyny in the room. Oh wait, I think that was coming from the mud.

"Kick the old broad in the boobs!" a young guy on my left shrieked.

"Ooops!" I pretended to slip, landing on my back with my foot driving into him hard directly under his chin. His head snapped back, and he dropped to the floor. This was more like it, I thought, getting back on my feet.

"That's a foul!" shouted his buddy, who for some reason didn't think it necessary to see if his friend was all right. "That stupid bimbo is a klutz!"

I feigned slipping again, grabbing him by the head and flipping him into the center of the pool. Caressa stayed there, still frozen in position and possibly time itself. She didn't move or blink as mud splashed on her. But I could swear she smiled a tiny bit.

"Hey!" The idiot pulled himself to his knees and wiped mud from his face. "She threw me!"

"Yeah," one of the bouncers on my right said. "You're not supposed to let customers into the pool."

"My bad." I smiled and walked over, picked the idiot up by his hair, dragged him to the side, and threw him over the edge. My knee *might* have connected pretty hard with his face. He joined

69

his pal as an immovable lump on the floor. A couple of guys stepped over them to get closer.

Valentine signaled me to get this underway, and I remembered I wasn't here to kick these chauvinist losers' butts. Although I could make that a part of my act...if I had one. At any rate, it was time, and I advanced slowly on Caressa.

She blinked.

Soon I was face to face with her. "Hi, um, I have a couple of questions..."

I didn't get to finish my sentence because somehow she pulled off a leg sweep that put me on my back. I hadn't seen that coming. Was the slow thing an act?

She gave an anemic war cry that reminded me of a slow-motion action scene in a bad movie where the volume is turned down. Caressa didn't jump on me so much as fall on me. It was a good thing I caught her or she might've really gotten hurt.

"I need to know about Delphine," I shouted in an attempt to drown out the cheering. "What can you tell me?"

Caressa seemed to snap out of it as her eyes attempted to focus on mine. "Crap dancer, lousy dolphin." She slowly wheezed before pushing off of me and getting to her feet. She landed an extremely weak kick to my abdomen that felt like I'd been hit with a wet paper bag.

"I win," she said. "Or no answers."

I gave her a quick nod and got to my feet. I had no qualms about not hurting her. I'd rather save my rage for the morons who surrounded the pool.

She threw a very weak punch and I pretended it landed. As I fake-reeled backward, I grabbed two guys who'd been making lewd remarks on either side of me and, as I made it look like I was scrambling to regain balance, brought their heads together hard like two coconuts. Then I tossed them each aside.

Caressa fell onto my legs in the worst takedown ever. I faked a backward fall into the mud.

"Good," she muttered as she loomed over me. "Delphine was a slut and a headcase. Believed in voodoo and thought everyone was conspiring against her."

That seemed like a juicy tidbit, so I didn't mind using my legs to help her get into a standing position. But what did it mean? Was it relevant to Delphine's murder?

I got to my feet as the men around me jeered.

"What a loser!" A fat, balding guy, who'd obviously never known the touch of a woman, snorted. "She's getting her ass handed to her by an old woman!"

I moved around the perimeter, my back to him, and reared my arm back like I was going to launch a punch at Caressa. My elbow connected with the side of his head...hard. Out of the corner of my eye, I watched him stagger back with a shocked look on his face.

The noise level faded a bit, and I noticed the spectators had taken a step back. I turned to my opponent and dove for her, trying to miss her by at least a few inches. She took the hint and with the speed of a comatose snail, moved one step to her right. As I landed on my stomach in the mud, I felt her foot come down on my back like a balloon hitting a pillow.

Caressa slowly lowered herself onto my back, every bone in her body creaking noisily. Finally, she sat and pulled my arms up behind me.

"Delphine wanted something I had," she hissed. "It kept her in her place. I hid it so she'd never find it."

I was kind of impressed. She'd said that without taking a breath.

So Caressa had something that kept Delphine in her place, and she'd hidden it. Could that be what Concepción thought her grandmother was going to steal? Was it the pearl from the pool? Why did Delphine want it, and how did it keep her in her place? Was it blackmail about the Spanish king's cousin?

Caressa dropped my arms and pressed down on my head,

forcing my face into the mud, where she held it. Even without any strength, it sent alarm bells through my body.

Nope. She doesn't get to kill me. I'd almost died so many times as a spy that getting killed in a pool of mud by a weak octogenarian would be humiliating. I got to my hands and knees and shook her off. Caressa landed on her back, and I helped her up. Once she was standing, I lifted her arm and declared her the champion to much catcalling and applause.

Two of the bouncers rushed over, wrapped the old woman in towels, and lifted her out of the mud. I headed for the edge of the pool and reached for a towel being offered by the woman who'd given me this ridiculous costume.

A young college-aged kid snatched it away. "That was lame! If you want this towel, you're going to have to take it off." His eyes raked my muddy form. "And I mean, all of it."

A huge cheer went up, and I smiled, wiping the mud from my face.

"Tell you what, Sport," I said. "Why don't you come in here and take it off of me?"

The kid turned triumphantly to his friends and shouted, "Hold my beer!"

His friends howled their support. Before the guy could turn to me, I grabbed his right arm and yanked, twisting it hard away from his body. The kid flipped sideways into the mud. I was on him in a second, pulling that same arm up and back with far more force than Caressa had used.

The kid turned his face to the side and squealed, "Help!"

I pulled his arm back even harder. I wasn't going to break or dislocate it. Well, I wasn't *planning* to do that. But the mud was slippery and he was a jerk, so all bets were off.

A couple of his friends advanced toward me.

"Don't do it," I warned. "Or not only will I rip his shoulder out of the socket, *you'll* be next."

The college guys held up their hands and backed away.

"Stop!" the kid wailed.

"Apologize," I insisted.

"I'm sorry! I'm sorry, okay?" Tears streamed down his cheeks.

I got off of him, and when he staggered to his feet I kicked him out of the pool.

"You cheated!" The big guy I'd hit with my elbow was holding a bottle of beer to his head. Then, he did something stupid. He called me the B-word.

I twisted his arm behind him, jacking the wrist up toward his shoulder blades and frog- marched him over to Valentine and Kate, who stood there, watching the whole performance.

"I saw you leering creepily at my friends while they were dancing." I hissed in his ear. "Apologize to the nice ladies."

"What? No! It wasn't me, lady, I—" This was followed by a scream as I jerked his hand higher up his back. "Okay, okay! I'm sorry! I'll never do it again! Please don't break my arm! It's my good gaming arm!"

Valentine and Kate accepted his apology, and I let him go. The other men looked at us uncertainly.

"Oh, I see! More of you wish to apologize for your bad behavior to these two ladies?"

They shook their heads and mumbled as they turned away.

Franki joined us. "Feel better now?" she asked me.

"Oh yeah. Much better." I looked down at myself. "Well, I did."

I was coated with smelly mud that was starting to dry. The feathers at the edge of the outfit were completely messed up, and some of the jewels and a lot of the sequins were missing.

"Your hair…" Valentine bit her lip, "…is going to need a bit of work."

"Did you find out anything?" Kate asked hopefully.

"I got some intel," I admitted. "But I have to find a shower before this all dries, or I'll be moving at the speed of Caressa."

In the dressing room, the dancers smiled and slapped me on

the back. Apparently, the guys I'd given mud baths to were not favorites.

"Here." One of the women handed me a fluffy bathrobe that had *The Saint* embroidered on it. "I swiped this from the maids for you."

"What size shoes ya wear, honey?" another woman drawled.

I told her my size and she grinned, handing me a pair of white canvas sneakers. "Just bought 'em, but after what you did, you can have 'em."

I thanked them and took a shower before climbing into the robe and shoes. It was nice to be clean and have comfy clothes. Hey, where were my clothes?

After asking around and discovering that no one claimed to have seen them, I wondered if the robe and shoes were actually considered a trade for my mermaid outfit.

"Merry!" Franki called into the room. "There's security footage!"

Yay! They could have my mermaid clothes. I ran out of the room and into the bar to see what my friends had discovered, hoping it'd be enough to free Jim.

Valentine and Franki were waiting. Kate apparently needed a bathroom break, but before she left she filled us in on her confrontation with Concepción in the dressing room and her surprise that the woman was even here.

I watched as she rushed to the bathroom, hoping she wouldn't be long so we could find out what was on the security footage.

"Where are your pants and top?" Valentine asked.

I shrugged. "No one in there has seen them. But this is comfy. And it has pockets!"

I reached inside the deep pockets and felt my cell as it started to buzz. I pulled it out, hoping my troop would never find out about my latest adventures in mud-wrestling.

A still shot of Caressa forcing me face-down into the mud popped up.

Too late.

No fair! You didn't let Betty wrestle alligators when we were in Louisiana! The text was from Betty, who apparently was referring to herself in third person now.

And I wouldn't let Betty mud-wrestle an elderly burlesque dancer either, I replied.

Lauren texted, *Now we have blackmail so you won't get us in trouble for doing what we did.*

Which is what, exactly? I wanted to know. If I was going to be blackmailed, it had better be for something good.

One of the Kaitlyns texted, *Ask her if the golden poison dart frog is still poisonous?*

Can we give him mouth-to-mouth? asked another.

What did you do to Rufus??? I demanded, hoping that three question marks demonstrated that I was angry.

And no, Rufus was no longer poisonous because he no longer lived in a rainforest and no longer ate the things that made him poisonous.

The video came through with the text *Proof of Life* and featured the frog bandaged so thoroughly I could only tell it was a frog by his shape and the one eye they hadn't managed to cover with bandages.

Rufus blinked in dismay. I knew just how he felt.

FRANKI

TRACI ANDRIGHETTI

"Everything okay, Merry?" I asked, keeping my distance while she stared at her phone. She looked like she'd swallowed a frog, but I didn't want to get too close after seeing her manhandle the audience.

Merry gathered the hem of her spa robe and sat at the bar. "Don't ask me how, but some of the girls in my troop got action shots of my kiddie-pool debut."

That was unfortunate since her costume had looked like Bert from *Sesame Street*—if he grew a beard and got glammed up with Miss Piggy's sequins and Big Bird's feathers. "We should see if your Girl Scouts can hack into the bar's security system," I said, half joking, "because Detective Mangiaratti won't let us see the footage."

Valentine slid onto a barstool. "It must have evidence about Delphine's murder."

I leaned against the bar. "According to Concepción, Delphine *did* come here before she went to the mansion."

Kate returned from the bathroom. "Don't go near the kiddie pool." She hefted her girth onto the stool next to Valentine. "They're looking for someone else to wrestle Caressa."

My eyes widened. "She's slow, but she's certainly got stamina."

A twenty-something male bartender pouring a beer on tap grinned at my comment. "Her secret is the Mudbug, a local drink named after her."

"What's that?" I asked. "A Coke spiked with amphetamines?"

"Close. Espresso and Campari."

It sounded disgusting, but given what it did for Caressa, it might be worth trying. I turned to Merry. "Speaking of the Mudbug, what did you find out while you were wrestling?"

"Not much. Caressa's lips were sealed as tight as pincers, but she did admit that she had something on Delphine."

That sounded promising. "Did you ask what it was?"

Merry gave me a wry look. "It was kind of hard while she was shoving my face in the mud. All I know is that she kept it hidden."

"Inside the pearl, I'm sure."

The bartender returned from delivering the beer. "Can I get you a drink?"

I waved him off. As much as I wanted to kick back and blow off steam with the girls, I had to stay focused on the case. "Did Caressa say anything else?"

Merry spun her stool to face me. "Just that Delphine was a slut for sleeping with a Spanish king's cousin."

Valentine placed her hand on Merry's arm. "And like I told Merry, his name was Eduardo, and he and Caressa were madly in love until Delphine stole him from her. Caressa was so distraught that she tied one on and trashed her dressing room. I heard this from the stagehand before my act."

I sucked my teeth. "Dolphins *are* known for stealing mating partners in the wild."

Valentine gave a hesitant smile as if wondering whether I was going to elaborate on the mating practices of dolphins. Figuring it was safe, she glanced from side to side and leaned forward. "And the stagehand was none other than Arthur."

"Arthur?" we all chimed.

"The guy Buddy and Tibs mentioned this morning after Jim was hauled away by the police. Probably figured he was too young to retire."

My text tone beeped, and I pulled my phone from my back pocket. "Glenda's outside."

I looked out the window overlooking Canal Street and saw a hand with a champagne flute beckoning to me from a limo. "Be right back."

I exited the hotel and climbed into the back of the car.

"*Bienvenidos*, Miss Franki." Glenda was keeping in theme with her stripper flamenco outfit—except for her French drink.

I glanced at the front seat. There was no sign of the driver. "How long have you been out here?"

She pointed her glass at the two Dom Perignon bottles on the limo bar before us. "Long enough to polish off one of the Doms, sugar."

"Is that why you didn't come inside?"

"That, and we've got to get you changed into your Tiger Eye costume." She held up tiger-striped scarves lined with purple in homage to the Louisiana State University mascot.

I hadn't seen the godawful getup since I'd worn it to catch a killer at Madame Moiselle's strip club. "No way I'm putting that on. You remember what happened last time."

"Indeed I do. You caught a tiger by the tail—a dastardly detective who tipped you five dollars, and your nonna decided he was a better beau than your Bradley."

"Which is another reason not to wear it again."

"You have to, sugar." She put down her half-empty glass and picked up a bottle. "You're overdressed for the Burgundy Bar."

That was stripper-ese for *Your shirt and jeans are too much fabric.*

She filled a second flute. "And it's the only way you'll wrestle any answers from my mother."

78

"You'd best be using *wrestle* figuratively." I reached for the glass.

She snatched it away and drained the champagne. "Getting info from that old woman is like pulling pearls from a clamshell. She's not going to talk unless she gets something out of it."

"Such as?"

"A show for her fans."

"Then I'll remind her she'll be putting on shows in prison if she doesn't help me clear her name." I grabbed the door handle, but Glenda's steely grip pulled me back.

"Hey! What the—"

"The show must go on, Miss Franki." She stripped off my clothes like she did her own when she performed. "And so must the costume."

I writhed and kicked, but my self-defense training from my rookie cop days was no match for her pole-dancing muscle or the wrestling moves she'd picked up from her mother.

Glenda stripped me bare and laid me across her lap, pinning me down with an elbow in my back. "Need I remind you that my mansion is a crime scene?" She wrapped my lady parts in a tiger scarf. "I won't get another renter until you solve that murder."

"It's a crime scene, all right," I said, face-down on the seat, "but you can't blame that on the killer."

She jerked my feet toward her and shoved on stripper shoes. Then she slapped my phone in my hand, kicked open the door, and shoved me onto the sidewalk. "Now get in that bar and catch another tiger."

It was fairly apparent that the caught tiger was me. Nevertheless, if I had to writhe in the mud to find out who killed Delphine, I would. Not for Glenda and her mother, but for Kate and Jim.

"The things I do to solve a case." I tottered toward the hotel in purple rhinestone platforms adorned with the LSU tiger and came to a halt. Beside the entrance was a newspaper vending machine. The *Times-Picayune* headline caught my attention.

Former King's Cousin Visits New Orleans.

Wait. Could he be the Spanish king's cousin whom Delphine stole from Caressa?

Dropping to a lap dance-style squat, I studied his picture. The distinguished, elderly gentleman would've been handsome were it not for a breathtakingly long nose. His name was beneath the photo, and it was as lengthy as his schnoz. Eduardo Francisco Pablo Victor Luis Maria Sanchez-Menéndez y de Borbón. "Yikes. Or maybe I should say, *Ay Chihuahua*. So *this* was Eduardo. No wonder they called him 'the former king's cousin.'"

According to the article, the Running of the Bulls had been moved from Saturday morning to late afternoon today to accommodate his schedule, and he was staying less than half a mile away at the Hotel Monteleone in the French Quarter.

A short guy drinking a Huge Ass Beer slowed to check me out. "Well, *grrr*," he purred. "Go get 'em, tiger."

I shot him the eye of the tiger and rose to my shoe-enhanced six-feet-four inches. "I will if you don't keep walking, pal."

He scampered off, and I waited until he was out of sight to tug at a scarf that was riding up. Then I dialed David's cell.

He picked up on the first ring. "Hey, Franki. Why'd you cancel Friday Lunch?"

My stomach gave a growl worthy of my costume, and I wondered whether Kate had polished off all the all-you-can-eat crawdads. "Sorry, David. Something came up, which is the reason I'm calling. I need you to get over to Hotel Monteleone and find out anything you can about the former king's cousin. A woman was found dead at Glenda's mansion, and she could be the mother of the child they'd once had together."

"Dude!" The exclamation was the apex of college-sophomore pathos. "I can be there in five. What's his name?"

My eye strayed to the newspaper, but the name was too much

to say aloud. "Just call him 'the former king's cousin.' They'll know who he is."

"Anything else?"

"Make sure Ruth told The Vassal to research Delphine and Caressa's fight at the 500 Club. I asked her to do that earlier, but knowing her, she didn't."

"On it. Uh…" He paused. "Ruth wants to talk to you."

"Sure, put her on." I hung up and went into the hotel lobby.

My phone rang.

I put it on silent.

It vibrated.

Despite my annoyance, I peeped at the text on the display.

You don't pick up, and I'll call Crime Stoppers and tell them you killed that decrepit dolphin.

Growling like a real tiger, I called David's number.

"You asked David about the former king's cousin," Ruth answered. "Well, I saw on the news that he came to town for business, not to fiesta. That restaurant and cantina on Freret Street, Mr. Tequila Bar and Grill, wants to use his name on their tequila."

"They must not know it because it's too long to fit on the bottle."

"Forget the bottle and focus on the booze," she barked, sounding a lot like her idol, Judge Judy. "A Mexican liquor for a Spanish king's cousin seems like a royal faux pas, doesn't it?"

"Royals regularly commit those. And maybe he's broke. The current king could have cut him off when the former king abdicated."

"I'm glad you brought him up. The man abdicated after he was accused of improper business deals." She harrumphed as loud as a gavel hitting a desk. "I say the cousin takes after him."

Too bad Louis Armstrong wasn't around. I'd love him to school her on hearsay, supposition, and slander. "You don't have any evidence that the tequila deal is crooked. And even if it were, I don't see what it has to do with Delphine's murder."

"Maybe nothing, but I smell a scam." She hung up.

The smell reference reminded me of the former king's cousin's sizable sniffer. As I crossed the hotel lobby, I pondered why the Spaniard would license his name to a product of Mexico. It did seem odd, especially considering that as a de Borbón, he was a better fit for a brand of bourbon. Still, I had no reason to connect his tequila deal to Delphine's death, particularly when she was killed at Caressa's ex-mansion.

I entered the bar and spotted Buddy and Tibs at a table near the stage. *What?*

I choked back a gasp, and my stomach lurched as though I'd just done a shot of mezcal with a worm.

How'd I miss those two, and why did they keep hanging around?

Tibs had complained that he and Buddy were has-beens. Were they trying to relive their heyday as bodyguards for the dancers? Or were they having trouble letting go of their girls?

Whatever their reason, it wasn't a good look when one of the women they used to protect had turned up murdered. I needed to have another chit-chat with the dubious duo.

"Looks like Franki's got a tiger in her tank."

My head jerked toward Merry's voice. She lounged in her spa robe at the bar, Sazerac in hand, grinning at my costume. Valentine had a cocktail too, a Pink Lady—sans booze, no doubt. Kate was snacking on the bar garnishes. Glad they were living it up while I was being assaulted in a limo by my ex-stripper landlady.

I scowled. "Ha. Ha."

Valentine giggled. "Easy, tiger."

The tiger jokes were getting as old as Caressa. But I couldn't change out of my stripes until I'd tussled with the crawdad.

Kate wolfed down a maraschino cherry and a martini onion. "What did Glenda say?"

Before I could answer, I had to untwist my lips from the horror of that garnish combination. "I'm going to have to wrestle her mudbug mother to get the dirt."

Valentine took a swallow of her virgin Pink Lady. "It won't be so bad now that Merry's taken out most of the spectators."

My gaze traveled to the kiddie pool, where Caressa stood as still as a corpse in her wrestling stance, towel over her shoulders. "It's not the spectators I'm worried about."

Merry smirked. "You'll be fine. Caressa might dress like a crawfish, but she's as gentle as a lamb."

I wasn't convinced. Based on my experience, the old crawdad was as wily as a coyote. But it was time to get on with the show. I kicked off my heels, did a few stretches, and headed for the wrestling pool.

Caressa hadn't moved a muscle. In fact, she was so stationary that I feared she really had passed, standing up. Then a corner of her mouth rose into a sly smile.

Valentine, Kate, and Merry whistled and whooped from the bar. I took a deep breath, set my phone on the floor outside the pool, and stepped into the slimy mud.

"Go, Tigers!" a guy screamed way too close behind me.

Startled, I slipped on the slick, murky bottom and landed on my back with a *thwack*. Dazed, I watched as Caressa put a muddy foot on my cheek in what seemed like slow-motion but wasn't. She hadn't even removed the towel from her shoulders.

A stagehand raised Caressa's arm in victory. "Give it up for the Crawdad Queen."

The audience roared at the short match.

The guy lifted Caressa from the pool and carried her in the direction of the dressing room.

And I didn't even get a lousy hand up! I tried to stand but slipped and fell back again. I wiped my eyes.

A pair of castanets hovered over my head.

"This is not the time to wallow in the mud, Miss Franki."

Glenda held up a cigarette holder loaded with a rose. "The bar is having a straddle-off, starting with the losers of the wrestling match."

"You can stop right there, Glenda. I'm not straddling anyone."

She put a hand on the ruffle that served as her skirt. "Get your mind out of the gutter, sugar."

I blinked. "I would, but I'm in a mud-wrestling pool in a bar where women take off their clothes."

Her thin lips pursed. "I was talking about the chair, not a man. Although the latter is certainly preferable." She pointed to a red velvet chair on the stage with a cross back. "Burlesque is all about the straddle and the strip."

I rolled to my knees, leaned over the edge, then snatched my phone and crawled out of the pool. "And I'm all about the shower and the scour because I'm sure people aren't the only things crawling in this mud. Where are my clothes?"

"In the limo, where you left them."

"Where *you* left them. I didn't undress myself, remember? Now please go and get them so I can lose these scarves." I stormed from the bar—carefully, so I wouldn't slip—not giving her time to refuse.

The dressing room was littered with feathers and plates of chicken bones. "What is this place? A graveyard for old hens?"

I located the showers, dropped my phone on a nearby chair, and rinsed off. Water was running in a neighboring stall, and I assumed it was Caressa. Just in case, I kept my costume on.

My phone rang, and I jumped out, hoping it was David. Sure enough. "Hey," I answered, "what have you got?"

"So, this is weird. One of the maids at the Monteleone said the former king's cousin can't speak Spanish."

"What?" I reached for a towel. "Surely he grew up in Spain?"

"I dunno. But, like, he told the maid's co-worker, who speaks English, that Mexican Spanish was too different from Castilian for him to understand."

84

And yet the guy is lending his mouthful of a moniker to a tequila brand. "That doesn't make sense. When I was at the University of Texas, I used my college Castilian Spanish in Cancun on spring break, and it worked *bueno*." I left out the part about said Spanish consisting of the food-and-drink words I read off menus since that wasn't relevant. "Keep digging on this guy, because something's up."

Caressa entered from the shower area buck naked, carrying her wig.

Stunned, I hung up. The crawdad queen had the body of a plucked chicken, head included. It was a traumatizing sight, which went perfectly with the décor of the dressing room.

Her bones creaked as she shuffled across the floor. When she arrived at her vanity, she slid on a pair of brown glasses, and her reptile eyes locked on me. "Child, you need to cover yourself."

Well, if that wasn't the chicken-and-dumplings pot calling the kettle black. But Glenda often said her burlesque-dancer mother was a prude, at least by stripper standards.

She pointed a bony finger at a coat rack. "Take that robe. It was a gift from my daughter."

I slipped on the white silk. It was cool on my skin, and drafty. "I came to—"

"I know why you're here." Caressa put on a robe, crawdad red, and lowered slowly into the vanity chair. Near her hand was a copy of the paper with the pic of the former king's cousin.

A coincidence? Or was she keeping tabs on him? I decided to sidestep that subject after learning from Valentine that his relationship with Delphine had once been the impetus for a dressing-room trashing. "Did Delphine come to the bar this morning?"

"Thought she was going to perform, the old whale."

"You mean, dolphin."

"No, she'd put on a pound or two, which is something we dancers can't afford to do." She set her rat's nest of a wig on top

85

of her head, and it sat there as though a bird had dropped it. "I saw to it that the performance was stopped."

"How? What did you do?"

"I didn't do a thing to Delphine. Didn't have to. She was her own worst enemy." She picked up a powder puff. "That woman could drink like a fish."

Dolphins are mammals, but I didn't point that out. The analogy worked given the context. "But she *was* murdered at your former mansion."

"And I have an air-tight alibi. The bar's security footage will show that I've been here the whole day."

"Okay, but she was there because of you."

Caressa's arm began a slow descent that eventually landed on the vanity with a hand-slam. "What do you want me to tell you? I didn't do it."

"You could start by telling me why you and Delphine didn't get along."

"She was a sloppy drunk who got into dancing late in the game. When she tried to break onto the scene, burlesque already had a mermaid, an oyster, and a crawdad. A dolphin was too much, not to mention it was all wrong for The Big Easy. An alligator, maybe."

I'd thought the same thing. "You had something on her that you kept in the pearl. What was it?"

"That, child, is between me and another person."

I was confused. "Delphine, right?"

"If you must know, Odette Malveaux."

My body went as rigid as a severed chicken foot. She was talking about a local voodoo priestess I knew all too well—and didn't want to know any better.

Caressa, who was no less rigid, but for an entirely different reason, threatened me with a snake-eyed stare. "You tell anyone, and you'll have to deal with her."

A knock shook me from my shock.

"*Entrez-vous*," Caressa called.

The door opened, and another stagehand who looked to be around eighty poked his head in the room. "Ready for your lift, my queen?"

She nodded. "Thank you, Arthur."

Arthur, huh?

The elderly man strode in, wearing pants and a short-sleeved shirt, a rope tattoo on his wrist catching my eye. He hoisted Caressa in his arms and carried her out.

And I'd thought he was talking about a car. Either way, it made me madder that I didn't get a hand from the pool.

My text tone beeped.

The Vassal had sent the research I'd requested. A photograph from a 1954 issue of the *Times Picayune*. It was clear that it had been taken the night Caressa destroyed Delphine's career by putting live crawfish in her dolphin pool.

The image showed a young Delphine reaching for her back—probably to remove a pinching crawdad—while an equally young Caressa laughed from one side of the stage. The caption below the picture identified a lone male onlooker as a Hollywood agent.

I zeroed in on his face and gasped.

The dressing room door opened, and Kate entered, followed by Valentine and Merry. "We just saw Caressa leave. Did you find anything to help Jim?"

I grabbed the newspaper from the vanity and held it up beside the picture on my phone.

The girls leaned in to look, and three sets of eyes popped.

They'd seen what I'd seen—the Hollywood agent was a younger version of the former king's cousin.

"Whoa!" Merry boomed. "Get a load of Cyrano de Bergerac."

Or maybe they hadn't. It was hard to get past his honker.

Kate took the paper. "Does this mean the former king's cousin once worked as a Hollywood agent?"

Valentine gave a thoughtful nod. "Some royals do have jobs."

"Oh, sure." Merry's tone was a tad sarcastic. "I mean, technically, the former Prince Charles worked as a farmer, but I don't think that's what's going on here."

I clicked my tongue, reflecting on this and our dubious dignitary who was in town for the annual event. "There's only one way to find out." I opened the dressing room door and gestured to my friends to follow me. "We've got to run with the bulls."

SURVEILLANCE FOOTAGE

ARLENE MCFARLANE

*I*NTERIOR - SAINT HOTEL LOBBY 8:55 a.m.

BACKGROUND MUSIC PLAYING "JOLENE" by Dolly Parton.

Grainy black-and-white video shows two elderly women arguing in a spacious hall beside tall, billowy white sheers. One woman is dressed in a crawdad-type burlesque costume. The other woman is dressed like a dolphin. The exchange is heated. Music too loud to make out conversation.

Crawdad woman raises both hands toward Dolphin woman in a choking-one-around-the-neck manner.

Dolly Parton continues to sing, asking Jolene how she could take her man.

Dolphin woman rolls her eyes at Crawdad woman and waves her hand down, then shuffles away.

Crawdad woman's eyes become large and angry. She shuffles out of the lobby on Dolphin woman's heels.

Lobby is empty. Sheers blow in the gentle breeze.

Dolly Parton finishes singing, begging Jolene not to take her man even though she can.

End: 8:58 a.m.

Cuts to a second video…

INTERIOR - BURGUNDY BAR 9:02 a.m.

TWO WOMEN, now identified as CARESSA the Crawdad Queen and DELPHINE the Dolphin Girl, shouting at each other beside a long bar. No other people in view.

CARESSA

You can't perform today. You're done in this town, you whale.

DELPHINE

Loosens her outfit from around her thick waist.

You're still holding a grudge from all those years ago.

Digs into her pocket, pulls out a phone, and holds it in front of CARESSA.

Take a good look, okay? That's Eduardo and me back in the day. And that's the baby we had. Get over it.

DELPHINE slaps her phone on the bar and turns back to CARESSA, pointing a finger in her face.

The years haven't been easy for me, and it's all because of you, you Craw-witch! Because Eduardo left you for me, you put a curse on me with your hocus-pocus. Don't think I haven't felt it.

CARESSA

CARESSA grins.

What goes around comes around.

She hobbles away.

DELPHINE stares open-mouthed at CARESSA's retreating back.

On the bar, the phone sits, forgotten. A gloved hand reaches up from behind the counter, clutches the phone, and slides it back behind the bar.

VALENTINE

ARLENE MCFARLANE

*W*e hurried out of the Burgundy Bar and jumped into Franki's Mustang, the mermaid doll Merry had handed me before her mud-wrestling act poking out of my bag, slightly worse for wear. Oh well. The hair show would be wrapping up by now anyway, and we'd clearly lost our chance at a prize. *C'est la vie.* There was always next year.

I let my gaze roam to Kate sitting next to me, her frizzy hair twice as wiry due to humidity, turning her poor head into a lion's mane. Maybe by the next hair show I could do something with her frizzled look…

She appeared deep in thought, as did the others, our next stop likely playing on everyone's mind. Right. The Running of the Bulls. What was this version like anyway? I mean, Spain's yearly heifer run sounded fun, but hadn't the odd person died during that event?

I was all of 5'4" and 118 pounds soaking wet. My idea of fun was slipping into a fancy dress and sparkly heels and dancing the night away. I still had lots of living—and loving—to do, not to mention a nutty salon to get back to. I had no intention of being

91

gored to death by a bull with a rusty ring through its nose—if they even wore nose rings.

I squared my shoulders and tightened my lips, defiant to the end. If I was going to meet a bull head-on, it'd better be trimmed in diamonds. Besides, I *had caught* more than a few crooks in my time. Only one had been the size of a bull, but none that I could think of had worn nose rings. And they'd all put up a good fight when they feared their freedom had been at stake...or was it because I'd tackled them with one of my beauty tools? A rascally grin slid across my face at that thought.

In any case, if I could lay my life on the line to seize a killer, then a little bull-running wouldn't stop me. At least with my friends by my side I'd be in good company. Bearing that in mind, I swept my hair off my sweaty shoulders and relaxed in the backseat.

The temperature had risen to hotter-than-hell, and we all— except for Franki—leaned our heads back, letting the warm breeze dry the perspiration dripping down our faces.

Kate popped her head up and broke the silence. "Guys, we were so focused back there on Caressa and Delphine's past affairs with Eduardo that I forgot to tell you I did something kind of devious."

Franki's gaze darted to the rearview mirror, and Merry whipped around from the passenger seat to face Kate and me, her remaining turquoise extensions resembling stringy seaweed.

"Don't hold out on us," she said. "What did you do?"

Now that Kate was back in her maternity clothes, she tugged her phone out of her sundress pocket and waved it in the air.

"You made a phone call?" I teased.

Kate flattened her lips. "No, silly. I taped the surveillance footage of Caressa and Delphine's argument in the Saint Hotel."

Franki screeched the brakes, missed sideswiping a car,

and swerved into a drugstore's parking lot. Then she threw the gear into Park and spun around. "You did *what?*"

Kate giggled, letting go of her death grip on my leg, and straightened back to her side of the seat. "I did. I'd just returned from the bathroom when I heard you tell Merry and Valentine that Mangiaratti wouldn't let us see this morning's footage. As luck would have it, when I exited the ladies' room, I spied him and the bar manager studying the recording in the manager's office. So I pulled out my phone, hid behind a potted plant, and filmed what they were watching."

"I *love* this girl!" I gave Kate's shoulder a quick squeeze. "You sure no one saw you taping it?"

Her eyes got big. "I don't think so. I did feel kind of spooked though. Then again, it might just be this whole case getting to me, and knowing Jim's rotting in jail."

I patted her hand. "He won't rot for long because the Four Musketeers are going to save the day!"

"Absolutely!" Merry cheered.

"Did you see anything suspicious or noteworthy in the footage?" Franki asked.

"I didn't actually watch the whole thing," Kate said. "I was too busy focusing on the backs of the manager's and Mangiaratti's heads, making sure they didn't turn around and spot me." She scooched forward and held the phone for us all to see, then clicked Play on the screen.

We watched in silence as Dolly Parton's voice was heard singing "Jolene" throughout the lobby while Caressa and Delphine yelled at each other, lips flapping, arms waving.

"Stop! Right there!" I said, after their fight had cut to the next scene inside the bar. "Can you rewind it?"

Kate quickly rewound the bar scene, then pressed Play again.

"What is it?" Merry asked. "I'm so fascinated by these two

dressed as fish and moving like snails, I can't focus on anything else."

Franki frowned. "I want to know what Delphine meant when she accused Caressa of putting a curse on her with *hocus-pocus*."

I darted my gaze from Franki back to the screen. "Stop! There it is." I gripped Kate's phone and held it for everyone to see. "Look, there. On the bar." I pointed to the right side of the screen.

"What *is it*?" Franki wrinkled her nose.

"Looks like a baby black octopus doing the mambo," Merry said, "which reminds me of the time I posed as a dancer in an Estonian strip club in this stringy black number..."

"That's not an octopus," I rushed out, not meaning to cut short Merry's Chechen strip-club story which ultimately would end with someone being stabbed, stunned, or stiffed. "It's a gloved hand, and it's stealing Delphine's phone."

I rewound it again, and we scrutinized it for a third time, witnessing Delphine set her phone on the bar. As she watched Caressa stalk away, a hand reached up and grabbed her phone.

"What we can't make out"—I studied the footage—"is whether it's a man's or a woman's hand."

"Whew," Franki whistled long and slow. "Who would've taken it?"

"And is it related to Delphine's murder?" Kate asked.

"I say we find out," Merry said.

"Wait." Franki held up a finger. "What time does the video read during all this?"

I scanned the film, zooming in on the numbers in the top left corner. "The first video in the lobby ended at 8:58 a.m., the second picking up in the bar at 9:02."

"What happened in those four minutes?" Kate examined the screen, as if looking for a smoking gun.

"My guess is, that's the time it took the two of them to trundle from the hallway into the bar." I scanned the phone, anyway, double-checking I hadn't missed anything.

Franki pressed her lips together, her cat-lined eyes narrowed. "Caressa had an air-tight alibi and swears the hotel's security footage will prove she was there all day."

"Which means she definitely couldn't have killed Delphine," I said.

"True." Merry grinned at the still frame of the stooped, elderly women. "If there was any doubt before."

I doggedly turned the events over in my mind, a growing sense that we were dealing with at least one falsehood. "If Delphine had dementia, as Concepción insinuated back at the mansion, she sure didn't display any signs from what we just witnessed."

"Also true." A contemplative look crossed Merry's face.

I'd been making a mental list of what we knew so far. The obvious had been considered. Now we had to look at the less obvious. "What about a name to go along with that Hollywood agent in Franki's photo? If Eduardo and the agent in the picture were one and the same, did Delphine know Eduardo was here? Had they remained in touch all these years?"

Franki smirked. "No name that I could see. But we know from the newspaper on Caressa's vanity that *she* was keeping up with Eduardo's comings and goings." She exhaled in a pensive manner. "Yet like you said, did Delphine know?"

I handed Kate back her phone and swept my hair to my other side, prying a stray pink feather off my damp shoulder bone. I blew it into the air, briefly thinking of my burlesque act.

A sudden image of Romero and his reaction to my steamy—albeit failed—performance came to mind.

A hot rush soared through me, picturing his fingers trailing down my cleavage, his dark whiskers tickling my neck as he came in close. I swallowed dryly. No question...he would've teased me and then—

"Something else..." Franki shifted in her seat, thankfully bringing me back to the present before the visuals became too steamy. "We have two part-time college students at Private Chicks who help us out on occasion. David and The Vassal."

We all scrunched up our noses at the last name.

"Don't ask," Franki said, moving on. "Before I got the photo from The Vassal, I'd asked David to do a little digging at the hotel our mystery man is staying at. Ends up, Eduardo, our infamous former king of Spain's cousin, can't speak a word of Spanish. Little ironic, don't you think?"

"That's a *lot* ironic," Merry said.

"And like saying the pope can't speak Italian," Kate added.

"Pope Francis speaks perfect Italian," Franki said, "and would have to in order to be the pope." She grimaced and shook her head. "And that old buzzard, Ruth, who also works in the office, said the real reason Eduardo's in town is because Mr. Tequila Bar and Grill wants to use his name on their tequila."

I chewed on my lip, taking this all in. "This keeps getting weirder and weirder."

"What's weird is the guy's got a name a mile long. Where do you suppose they're going to fit *that* on the label?"

"If that *is* his name." I reflected on this some more.

"By the way..." Kate shoved her phone back in her pocket, "where did Buddy and Tibs get to?"

Franki put the car in Drive and careened out of the lot. "Who knows?"

Kate pressed on. "Do you think they're following us? I mean, they were also just at the club."

"I wouldn't rule anything out." Franki glanced at us in the rearview mirror. "There's something about those two..."

"Yeah," Merry agreed. "The way they're slinking in and out of the picture, they would've made perfect FBI agents."

I held back a giggle, recalling FBI Agents Summer and Winter from our previous case. I didn't want to raise the point, but if

Buddy and Tibs ended up as "perfect" as those two, we were in trouble.

MINUTES LATER, we arrived at a crowded, blocked-off street filled with hundreds of runners, dressed in white with red scarves. A banner that read RUNNING OF THE BULLS swayed high across the festivities from one pole to another. Jazz music blared in the background.

Waiting for the signal to start the chase were roller derby girls, dressed as cute bulls in red and black, foam baseball bats poised to playfully beat runners. I smiled, watching them stomp their roller hooves, their adorable horned helmets aimed forward.

Now *this* looked fun! Suddenly I pictured Romero roguishly swatting me with a foam bat. After all, he *had* said on more than one occasion that he'd like to put me over his knee.

I choked back a cough. On second thought, this was more up my sexy employee Jock de Marco's alley. I mean, Spanish *was* his first language.

I fanned myself at the racy notions and peeled another left-over feather off my shoulder as the announcer's voice interrupted the jazz music, urging everyone to get ready to start.

This quieted the throng to a dull roar. The mood was set to *happy* on account of drunks getting a head start on the festivities, but I'd seen mobs like this before. *Happy* could turn to *ugly* all because one guy looked at another guy's girl.

The four of us gave each other a subtle group nod, an unspoken understanding among friends on a mission. Then we cased the crowd.

Merry pulled on the lapels of her white bathrobe as if it were a trench coat and she was in CIA mode. "Where's this fraud supposed to be?"

"I don't know." Franki spun around, searching the grounds. "But if he's as important as he's pretending to be, he's probably sitting as guest of honor somewhere, wearing a sash and fake medals. We should blend into the masses and start looking."

Ha. *Us* blend into a crowd? Merry looked as though she'd just walked out of a sauna, I resembled a half-plucked, pink-feathered Chicken Little, Kate looked like she was ready to pop, and Franki had a peekaboo thing happening at the rear of her robe. We'd blend into a crowd about as much as Canadian Prime Minister Justin Trudeau blended into a sea of bald men.

"Uh, Franki?" I pulled her back by the silky arm of her white robe before she went too far. "Do you find it a bit drafty down there?"

Before I got all the words out, she instinctively patted her behind. "Damn. I *have* been finding it drafty." She peeked over her shoulder and whirled around like a cat chasing its tail. "What did that crusty old crawdad give me to wear?"

I wasn't sure how to tell her that a big, holey appliqué of a famous band's red-tongue-and-lip logo was sewn to her robe. "From the look of it, I'd say it's something to honor the Rolling Stones."

Kate and Merry snickered.

"*What?*" Franki attempted to pull the hem around so she could see what was plastered on her derrière. "I should've known Glenda would give her ninety-year-old mother something risqué to wear."

To be helpful, I dug out my compact mirror and angled it behind her so she could get a better look.

Franki's brows went up in horror. "That pain in the—"

Suddenly a thunderous blowhorn sounded, drowning out her words and signaling the start of the chase.

"Come on!" Franki released the hem, forgetting about her indecency. "We need skates."

I wasn't missing this for the world. I hadn't been on roller skates since the time my childhood friend Babette Lang and I pretended we were in Elton John's band. We roller-skated around our driveways, singing "Bennie and the Jets," boa feathers trailing from our necks, huge colorful star-shaped sunglasses perched on our youthful cheeks.

We finished lacing up, and Franki led the way. She snatched a stray red scarf off a bench and, without breaking her stride, wove it through the cut-out on her rump. This only added to the look and made the tongue flicker grossly, but I let it go. There were more important things at stake.

"Uh..." Kate stammered, peering down at her skates. "I might need help."

I gave her a soft nudge. "You sure you want to do this?"

She nodded defiantly. "I'm one of the Four Musketeers, remember? You're not leaving me behind! Anyway, we need to find the elusive Señor Eduardo!"

Merry's fair eyebrows disappeared under her blue curls at Kate's boldness, and I smiled encouragingly. "You know best. We'll help you."

I motioned for Merry to flank Kate's other side. She nodded, and we scooped our arms under Kate's elbows, lifted her an inch off the ground, and pushed forward into the crowd, searching for Eduardo.

Feeling tall in my roller skates, I poked my head toward Merry. "Want to tell us how the Estonia strip-club story ended?"

Merry grinned, keeping in time to my pace, Kate securely between us. "Oh, right. The leggy fringe on that stringy black number I wore came in handy."

"For what?" Kate asked, gliding along between us.

"Strangling a Russian spy."

Kate gawked from me to Merry. "Did he die?"

Merry shrugged, her remaining hair extensions bopping on her robed shoulders. "I'm not allowed to disclose that. But I *will* say the guy won't be drinking any more vodkas on the rocks."

The announcer's booth was in sight, nothing more than a tall lean-to on stilts with huge speakers on either side, rows of bleachers below.

"Here's our chance." I squinted up at the booth in direct line with the sun. "Can you see anyone resembling the man in Franki's photo?"

"Yeesh!" Merry squawked. "The sun's making it hard to see who's inside that stall."

"Looks like someone just got 'horned,'" the announcer joked, clearly about the runner twenty feet in front of us who was holding his backside, fleeing a "bull."

"Wait!" he said. "What's this approaching? Looks like a blue-crab sandwich. Something of a delicacy around here." He laughed, his broadcasting voice rich and deep. "Actually, it's more of a blue-*whale* sandwich."

"Of all the—" Kate sputtered, making fists with her pudgy hands. "He's talking about *us!*"

"Nonsense." I continued my stride, abandoning my search of the announcer's box to glance down at Kate. "You don't look anything like a whale." It wasn't the biggest fib I'd ever told.

"*Yeah!*" Merry agreed heartily. The one time one of her anecdotes would've come in handy, and she failed to come up with a pleasing comparison for what Kate *did* look like.

"Hey!" Kate stiffened and stumbled in her tracks. "That woman just swiped my phone from my pocket!"

"What woman?" Merry tore her gaze through the swarm of people.

"Up there. I think she's in red."

That narrowed it down to a thousand.

"I'll waterboard her when I catch her," Merry said.

We picked up speed, Kate almost airborne between us.

"There!" Kate pointed, her elbows still secure in our hands. "She's getting away."

"Which woman is it?" I asked. "With everyone in white

and red, no one stands out."

"She's up by Franki. See her? She has brown hair."

"Mahogany brown? Chestnut brown? Or golden brown?" I couldn't help it. Hair was my profession.

"I don't know." Kate huffed in anger. "First Delphine's phone is nabbed, now mine."

Merry dropped Kate's arm and zoomed ahead, shouting back over her shoulder. "Franki and I will get it."

An obese guy with a drink in his hand staggered toward us, opposite the crowd, like a salmon swimming upstream. He came to a sudden stop, swaying on his feet as if crashing to the ground was next on his agenda. He belched in our faces and glared at Kate. "You really shouldn' race in yer condishun."

Interacting with drunks was high on my Things-I-Hate-Most list, but I wasn't going to let an extremely pregnant woman handle this herself. I almost remarked, *In your condition you shouldn't be drinking...or standing...or breathing*. Instead, I wheeled toward him and raised a lethal brow, which always worked on Max and Phyllis when words were futile.

He shifted his bloodshot, heavy-lidded eyes from Kate up to me and slurred his next words. "Who're you?"

I swallowed back his rank odor, yanked Ariel from my bag, and pressed her pointy feet into the soft spot inside his left shoulder. Using the right force, this could bring a man to his knees. I'd learned that firsthand when I'd taken karate on a whim a year ago and a tiny Asian instructor demonstrated this move on me using only his thumb. Irritating little guy.

"You ever heard of Lara Croft: Tomb Raider...or Wonder Woman?" I strengthened my stance, twisting Ariel's feet into his shoulder for effect. "I've been compared to both."

It was a brave thing to say even if it happened to be true. The guy had a hundred pounds on me and could've easily lifted me with one hand, twirled me in the air, and tossed me into the crowd.

If I was going to act tough I figured I should use any backup I had. "Now run along and join the fun, okay?" If this guy had any more fun, he'd laugh himself to the morgue.

Seeing as he was a dozen sheets to the wind, he gave us a happy-drunk shrug and staggered away, looking for the next victim to harass. On his heels, two derby girls wheeled by and screeched their brakes, their jaws dropping at the sight of me clutching Ariel, the poor mermaid's hair looking worse than Merry's, if that was possible.

"It's not mine!" I said before they shook their horned helmets and sped away. "It was a prop for a hair show!" I cried out after them. Sheesh. Didn't bulls have any imagination?

I dumped Ariel headfirst back in my bag and blinked at Kate, getting back on track. "Why would anyone swipe your phone? Unless...you sure nobody saw you film that footage."

Her hand covered her belly, the expression in her eyes strained. "Pretty sure." She dabbed a stream of sweat running down her temple, then leaned over a nearby fountain for some water.

"Things are going from bad to worse." She swiped the back of her hand across her chin. "Jim's going to grow old in that jail. He won't even see the birth of the twins if we don't solve this case and set him free."

I rubbed her arm, an impulsive act I did with people I liked. "He'll see the birth." Listen to me. Like I had all the answers.

I had to get her attention off Jim and back to the festivities. "Look, Merry and Franki will find your phone. In the meantime, if there's something strange about the former king of Spain's cousin, I want to see it firsthand. You with me?"

She nodded.

I removed another stray pink feather from my cleavage and let it float to the ground. "Come on. Let's find out who this guy Eduardo really is."

KATE

DIANA ORGAIN

o Do

1. Get Jim out of jail.
2. Call mom and check in on Laurie…ugh, first get my phone back.
3. Figure out who this Eduardo guy really is.
4. Feed the twins. (Again, really?)
5. Ride a steamboat.
6. Take the Haunted History vampire tour. (Will there even be time for this?)

I had a bad feeling in my gut.

I wished it was only the twins doing cartwheels or kicking my ribs, demanding to be fed again, but something told me our disastrous New Orleans vacation had taken a turn for the worse.

Who'd just nabbed my phone?

Not for a nanosecond did I believe it was a random act. That I was merely a distracted pickpocket victim in a crowd. Someone had targeted me on purpose.

Maybe Valentine had been right. I'd been spotted videotaping the security footage.

Even though I'd concealed myself behind a potted plant, what were the chances no one saw my big preggo belly sticking out?

Slim to none.

Who knew we were here? Right. Buddy and Tibs!

Goosebumps pimpled my arms at the thought. But could one of them really have been sly enough to steal my phone? It seemed unlikely.

My phone!

I hated the feeling of being without it. What if my mother was trying to reach me? What if there was an emergency with Laurie? I'd have no idea that my baby was in trouble. And what about Jim? He'd already made more than one phone call from jail. What if he was trying to reach me again with a break in the case?

I wiped those thoughts away and quelled the nervousness I felt about not being in touch with my family. I had to trust that Franki and Merry would recover my phone. After all, I'd gone through the trouble of password-securing it. Even if someone *had* stolen it, I didn't think they'd see the surveillance footage from the bar.

My thoughts rolled back to who it could be. If not Buddy and Tibs, then who? Was there someone else at the bar who could've been interested in Delphine's murder? Before I ruminated further on this, Valentine touched my shoulder.

"You ready to meet Eduardo?"

I shaded my eyes with my hand and glanced at the announcer's booth on stilts. The rows of bleachers were definitely packed. If the former king's cousin was here, there was a good chance he was seated in that section holding a cold beer—or a tequila.

To say my mouth watered was an understatement. The air was so humid, I felt like I was skating inside a swimming pool. Could my shuffling along in these skates even be called skating?

"Hey," I said to Valentine. "Let's find a place so I can get these off my feet. I'm already a hazard *without* wheels."

Valentine nodded, too kind to say anything further about how ridiculous I must look in skates. "Let me go back and grab your shoes." And she was gone and back in a flash, my comfy, spongy flats sticking out of her bag.

On our way over to the announcer's booth, we passed a hot dog stand with a long line of people who had *hangry* looks on their faces. I sympathized, and my stomach growled.

I glanced again at the serpentine line.

Would Valentine let me grab a quick hot dog?

I turned to her, but she had such a determined look on her face I didn't want to risk it.

The twins somersaulted against my belly as if they could smell the all-beef hot dogs slathered with sauerkraut and onion.

I bit my lip and refocused. As we approached the lean-to for a spot to sit, I realized there was a live radio broadcast taking place with a bright "ON AIR" light flashing. Before I could indicate this to Valentine, she poked me in the ribs.

"There he is!"

Seated next to the announcer was a man who appeared to be Eduardo. There was really no mistaking that nose! He stood and shook hands with the radio announcer as if just finishing an interview, then stepped down from the booth.

Valentine handed me my shoes and then pounced on him. "Excuse me," she said, batting her eyelashes. "Got a minute?"

The man looked Valentine up and down appreciatively. "I always have a minute for a pretty lady. Besides, I think it's time for a break." He wiggled his bushy gray eyebrows at her. "Can I interest you in a cold drink? A tequila maybe?"

Valentine smiled. "Ah. Tequila. A favorite of yours?"

"But of course."

"Especially when you're going to be a representative for Mr. Tequila Bar and Grill."

Go Valentine!

She paused for effect. "You're Eduardo Francisco, uh..."

The man puffed his chest out bigger than Foghorn Leghorn. "Eduardo Francisco Pablo Victor Luis Maria Sanchez-Menéndez y de Borbón."

While he and Valentine chatted, I glanced around for a safe spot to tear the skates from my feet. I hated to miss the chance to grill him, but Valentine seemed to have him eating out of the palm of her hand. The bleachers were home to a rowdy, drunk crowd, and the only empty spot was the one Eduardo had just vacated.

I trudged up the steps, gripping the handrails for dear life, and plopped onto the seat next to the announcer to undo my skates.

The man next to me turned, a little surprised to see someone other than Eduardo sitting beside him.

"Hi," I said. "I'm just here for a minute, taking off my skates."

"No problem," he said, a bit unsure. "Where did George go?" He looked over my shoulder to where Eduardo and Valentine were giggling conspiratorially.

George?

"Aha. The old devil." He grinned, focusing from Eduardo and Valentine below back to me. "Go ahead. Give us your best shot. I need a break."

"Give us your best shot about what?"

"Announce!"

I looked horrified at him. Certainly, he didn't expect me to do a play-by-play call of the event.

"We're live on radio." He pointed to a red button by my mic. "Come on. Your mic's about to go on. The commercial's ending."

I stared at him, startled. "No, no. I just need the skates off!"

My red light turned green.

"And coming to you live from New Orleans is..." He looked at me expectedly.

"Kate Connolly," I said with hesitation.

106

"Wonderful, Kate. You're visiting here at the Running of the Bulls, from where?"

"San Francisco."

"And what do you think of our festivities?"

"It's certainly unique," I said, finding my courage. "I've always wanted to go to the Running of the Bulls in Spain. I guess this is the next best thing."

He chuckled. "Of course. What more could you want? We've got white costumes and red sashes. Red wine's flowing. Beautiful bulls. No one's going to die from being gored today."

I laughed nervously. "That's right. Quite an interesting take on an old tradition. And no bulls will be killed either."

He grinned at me reassuringly. "Or matadors! Only good fun here in New Orleans. Tell us, what brought you to The Big Easy?"

I did a quick rundown in my mind. I couldn't very well tell him about Delphine's murder or Jim being in jail, but I managed to find a truth I could share. "I'm here visiting friends," I said, "before the babies come."

"As this is radio, you'll have to expand for our audience." He chuckled. "Just don't expand too much."

What? Before I could ask him to clarify, he continued. "My companion here looks like she's nine months pregnant with twins."

"No," I said, annoyed. "Six."

His eyes widened. "You're having *six* babies?"

"No! I'm six months along." Good Lord, what was wrong with this man?

He sighed. "Being pregnant is certainly a labor of love. My dear wife birthed six."

It was my turn for my eyes to widen. "You have *six children*?"

"Yes. Brandon, Brandy, Bailey, Ben, Bridget, and Beverly."

He'd stunned me into silence.

I was having a hard time imagining Jim handling our upcoming three kids. How did a family handle six?

"What's been the highlight of your New Orleans trip?" he asked.

Again, I floundered for words. Jim's arrest and the murder investigation weren't really highlight material. "Um. Earlier, we ate mudbugs at a place on Canal Street."

"Lovely. There's stellar adult entertainment on that street." He gave me a lascivious look, and I knew I'd said the wrong thing.

Suddenly, in front of us, a roller girl gored a near-naked man with her plastic horns. He screamed in delight, flipped back, and knocked into her, causing a pile up of falling roller girls.

The announcer perked up, taking his attention off me, calling out a play-by-play of the ruckus.

I used this opportunity to slide on my shoes. As I made my exit, he went to commercial break, then called after me. "Hey, when you're down there, please send George back up."

I stopped short and pivoted back to him. "Why do you keep calling him George?"

The announcer grimaced. "Oh. I meant Eduardo."

"No, you called him George, twice. I may be six months pregnant, but I still have my hearing."

He bit his lip, then let out a breath. "Okay. Between you and me, I overheard a woman call him George Roscoe. He looked around nervously and then corrected her. But if you ask me, he acted like a guy who'd been caught in a lie."

"How did the woman react when he corrected her?"

He shrugged. "She apologized rather loudly and said she thought she'd recognized him from a long time ago."

Had she? Or was the former king's cousin an impostor?

I hustled off the platform and walked toward where Valentine and Eduardo were still chatting.

"Kate!" Valentine said, the expression on her face indicating she was happy to see me.

"Hey." I turned to Eduardo. "George, the announcer would like you to return."

Valentine frowned and stared at me.

The former king's cousin froze.

"You *are* George Roscoe, aren't you?" I asked.

"You must have me mistaken for someone else, *señora*," he said in a Spanish accent as fake as he was. He spun on a heel and bounded up the steps back to the booth.

I turned to Valentine.

"His name is George Roscoe?" she asked.

"Apparently. It looks like he got that nose in true Pinocchio fashion."

MERRY

LESLIE LANGTRY

I hadn't been on roller skates since the Kadryov Goat Derby in Chechnya. Every warlord entered a skater, and since I'd been the only one of Azlan's "men" who didn't agree with the general consensus that skates were tiny cars for weasels, it was up to me. The event took place on a rotting and rusted playground littered with broken glass—or as it was known there, the nicest playground in Chechnya. Each team had a makeshift goat pen, and skaters got to keep every goat they dragged to that enclosure. Sounded easy, right?

There was a catch. Actually, there were two. First, the goats were also on skates and, even though he always denied it, Kadryov, pathetic despot that he was, trained them to skate away from people. If you miraculously managed to chase down and drag a goat to your pen, it was too soon to celebrate. The goats were wearing suicide vests that you had to defuse before you could get another goat.

Fortunately, my CIA background worked in my favor as I'd had some experience defusing bombs. There were a few other guys in the competition who managed to pull it off, but in the end there weren't as many competitors...or goats...as we'd started out with.

I was able to capture six goats, which was great because goats are better than currency in most parts of Chechnya. Azlan awarded me with six bottles of Panamanian vodka, which was also considered currency since the local stuff was so bad it either made you devastatingly incontinent for a month, or permanently blind with a temporary spitting problem.

As I'd skated away from Valentine and Kate to catch the thief who'd stolen Kate's phone, I snagged two helmets from a table. Safety first! I reached Franki, handed her the helmet, and told her what had happened, including the part about the skater with brown hair.

"Was she a bull or a runner?" Franki put the helmet on and adjusted the strap.

"A bull, I think." I bit my lip. "It was hard to tell from where Kate was pointing, but I think she was a bull."

We both took off in the direction of dozens of brunette bulls.

Unfortunately, the street was packed. Getting through was like racing chest deep through Jell-O—which happened on the second day of the Kadryov Goat Derby. I wasn't as successful in that event, but at least there were no bombs involved. Sadly, lime Jell-O is impossible to get out of blonde hair, so be forewarned to Jell-O-race at your own risk.

Franki pointed. "There's the one with the phone!"

There was only one woman in red wearing skates who was also holding onto a phone. I was right. She was a bull in a red shirt, black shorts, and a helmet decorated with two French horns as...um...horns. We could only see her from the back, and then only in slivered glimpses.

"Roller derby girls." Franki craned her neck. "Our thief is one of the French Whorens. Watch out! Those ladies play rougher than most."

Sure enough, French Whorens was printed on the back of her

shirt. Franki had pronounced it as *horns*. It reminded me of home, where the Who's There school team was called The Fighting Whorish—an unfortunate combination of the town's name and the nationality of those who'd settled there. At least it wasn't as bad as our bitter rivals from nearby Bladdersly, who were known as The Raging Bladders.

I shouted to be heard over the din. "We'll never get her this way! I'll go up the right on the outside! You take the left. When we get ahead of her, we'll come at her from both sides and snag her like a Chechen goat!"

Franki gave a short nod as if this wasn't a weird thing to say and sped off while I skated to the right. I caught brief sightings of the French horn helmet we were stalking as she darted in and out through the crowd. She wasn't swinging her bat at anyone, which made me think she was too busy trying to escape with Kate's phone.

Poor Kate! She'd really been through the ringer today. First Jim was arrested, then she'd gone too long without food, and now her phone had been swiped! Her whole life was probably on there, along with photos of her toddler back home. Currently, my phone was filled with terrifying nonsense from my troop. For a split second, I wondered if losing my phone wouldn't be a blessing at the moment.

I gained speed, glancing occasionally over at Franki, when I could see her. The two of us were side-by-side, albeit separated by a whole street full of drunken revelers. We were gaining on the thief, but not by much. The packed crowd was tough to get past as they eagerly awaited being smacked by a foam ball bat.

At least it wasn't the annual Dear-Leader-Began-Driving-At-Age-Three Celebration Day in Pyongyang, where hopeful North Korean parents flooded the streets putting their toddlers behind the wheel in order to match this extremely ridiculous claim. That was one occasion where it was best to be off the streets or, better yet, out of the country entirely.

"Looks like Booty Bull and Spa Bull are playing offensive offense!" the announcer shouted.

Did he mean Franki? She was showing off some booty. I must be Spa Bull, dressed in the Saint Hotel's plush robe. I caught a glimpse of Franki grimacing. She must've heard it, too.

So we were considered bulls, huh? That seemed unfair since we didn't have foam bats. I could really get people to move if I had one of those. Oh sure, they were light and harmless. But as Valentine had shown, anything could be used as a weapon depending on how you deployed it. I once saw an MI6 agent kill an ISIS terrorist with a paper towel. He was so efficient that after he killed the bad guy, he used it to clean up after. It was very absorbent.

"Look at Booty Bull go!" the announcer shouted. "Spa Bull has her work cut out to catch this cheeky bovine!"

Franki had found an open sidewalk, jumped the curb and was racing ahead. My sidewalk was blocked. I needed a strategy so I could catch up and help her take this thief down.

Then I heard it. Several *ayooogah* horn blasts made me turn to see a very old woman, dressed as a bull, zipping up behind me on a motorized cart. The wizened wonder bull wore a tight red T-shirt and a red-glittered helmet with horns made out of the plastic lacing my troop used for lanyards. She was pounding the horn to get people out of the way, and they were diving right and left. As she passed me, I grabbed the back of her seat and hitched a ride.

"Wheeeeeee!" the elderly racer cried out. She turned around and spotted me. "A new friend!"

At least that's what I think she said.

"I need your help!" I shouted. "Some chick stole my pregnant friend's cell phone!"

The woman stared at me over her shoulder, violently ramming into people because she wasn't watching where she was going. We hit about five in rapid succession, and she didn't seem

113

concerned. Every time she hit someone, the scooter made a *thunk*.

Thunk. "Name's Naughty Nola!" she shrieked as she hit a young couple in white T-shirts. *Thunk. Thunk.*

"Another burlesque dancer?" I blurted. *Thunk*.

She shook her head. *Thunk*. "No! Not Naughty! *Knotty*! I'm the oldest living Girl Scout in New Orleans, and I'm very good with knots!" *Thunk*.

"I'm Merry!" I shouted back. "A Girl Scout leader from Iowa!"

The pruney face split into a wide smile. *Thunk. Thunk*. "All right! Let's get this thief!"

She turned around and hit the pedal, sending us into warp speed. My head snapped back as we took off. What did she have on this thing—rocket engines? I looked down to see sparks shooting off my skates.

This seemed like a bad idea, especially as my robe blew open below the belt, revealing more than Booty Bull. I reached down with one hand and held the robe closed. I toyed with letting go with the other, but we had to be doing at least 25 mph, and since I didn't want to spend the rest of my time here in a hospital in traction, I decided against that idea.

"I've lived here all my life!" Nola shouted. "Never was a bull before. Now I get to do that and stop a thief!"

We were going so fast, I was fairly certain we'd passed Franki and the thief a long way back. We burst through the front of the runners and raced a few blocks further before I could stop her.

"PULL OVER!" I shouted.

Nola slammed on the brakes, and I flew forward over her head, landing on the ground in front of the scooter.

The woman frowned. "You'd best put some panties on, Scout!"

I quickly covered up as I climbed to my feet. "Sorry about that. We were at the Burgundy Bar, and someone made me mud-wrestle Caressa the Crawdad. My clothes were a mess, so they gave me this to wear."

Nola whistled. "You're a long way from the Burgundy Bar. Did you say you wrestled Caressa the Crawdad?"

I nodded as I ran my hands through my wind-blown hair. It was quieter here. There were a lot of tourists on the sidewalk waiting for the runners and bulls to appear.

"I hope you kicked her tail." Nola shook her head. "That woman is vicious. Especially after what she did to Delphine the Dolphin Girl."

My *spy*-dy senses tingled.

"Delphine?" I asked. "Did you know she was murdered?"

Nola's mouth dropped open. "What? How? Who did it? Was it Caressa? That woman truly hated Delphine. Did you know she once put Nair hair remover in Delphine's shampoo bottle? And then there was that time she put Icy Hot on the dolphin's G-string. In all my years, I never heard anyone make a sound like that!"

"Caressa has an alibi." I brushed the remaining curls out of my face. "We don't know who killed Delphine. My friend's husband was arrested for the murder, but he didn't do it."

Knotty Nola stared at me for a moment. "Well, if I were you, I'd look into Buddy and Tibs. They were obsessed with Delphine to the point she was thinking of getting a restraining order." She revved the motor on her scooter. "And those men were Boy Scouts…if you know what I mean." The elderly woman winked and then tore off straight ahead.

As she zoomed away, I realized I needed to get back to the action to help Franki. The tip on Buddy and Tibs was interesting. Boy Scouts could be diabolical. My troop had had to put them in their place more than once. In fact, my troop had a lifetime ban from any Boy Scout event in a two-county radius. I'd be lying if I said I wasn't a little proud of that.

Hearing the roar of the crowd heading my way, I started to

skate back toward it. Perhaps I'd run into the thief head on. Tourists edged the street, many looking at me curiously as if I were the pregame entertainment.

A woman about ten feet away turned and vanished into the crowd, leaving a hair clip in the gutter. I scooped it up and used it to hold the bottom of my robe together before skating back into the direction of the mob.

The runners came at me en masse, and I fought my way through the crowd, looking for the woman with the French horns. Finally, I spotted one. No, wait, there were five. Well, one of them had to be the thief. I looked for Franki but didn't see her.

I skated toward the women, who looked me up and down. They were all brunettes with athletic builds, and I had no idea if one of them had taken Kate's phone. I let them pass me by and spun around to follow them. Not one of them had a phone in her hand. But since they had the same hair and musically inspired, prostitute-suggestive helmets, I decided to check them out. It was possible the phone was in a pocket.

They seemed to be waiting for me. As I neared, they parted in the middle, letting me through. Then they pounded me with their bats. Hard.

"Why are you eyeballing us?" one of them snapped.

"I saw her and another girl earlier!" another cried as she whacked me on the legs. "She was chasing La Dauphine!"

"Get her!" said another, who tried to kneecap me with her foam bat.

"Hey!" I snatched one of the bats and swung it around. "Stop hitting me! I'm just looking for a pickpocket who was dressed like you!"

"Are you accusing us of stealing?" an outraged brunette shouted.

She smacked me on the hip. She swung again at my head, but I managed to block her bat with mine. This woman wasn't going to give up anytime soon.

"Not you, necessarily..." I responded with an uppercut via foam bat. It clipped her on the chin, brought her head back, and she fell to the ground.

Another bull swung her bat toward me, but not before I rammed the end of mine into her abdomen, causing her to double over.

There were two remaining skaters because the third skated away. She must be the one with the phone! I took off after her with the other two hot on my wheels.

Both of those French Whorens caught up and slammed into me on either side. It hurt, but I shrugged them off and fled after the other skater, wondering if Franki was somewhere nearby.

None of these skaters looked familiar, which made me question if the thief was someone who saw an opportunity and took Kate's phone. Who stole phones anymore?

Considering all the apps to track your device, why would anyone steal one? It would have to be because you wanted something on that particular cell, or you were doing it for kicks.

The escaping French Whoren was just ahead. Maybe the rest were protecting her. I started to speed up when I felt a tug on my robe. The two bulls behind me were holding onto my robe, and it was in danger of coming off. The only thing keeping me from being called Naked Bull were my hands clinging to my lapels.

Where was Franki? Maybe she found the real thief and was back in the crowd with her. Risking literal exposure, I hit my toe stop.

The two skaters flew ahead, each dropping my robe. I skated to catch up to them. They were about to turn around when I caught each one by an arm and slammed them into each other. They bounced away from the other, a little dazed. It only took a minute before they lunged at me, fists flying.

I had to admit, I was in trouble. These women were trained at fighting on wheels, and that was a bit outside my skill set. I couldn't hold them off much longer. The bulls brought their fists back, telegraphing that I was about to get clocked in the jaw on both sides. I ducked, reached down, and grabbed each woman by one ankle. Then I tugged upward, hard. The two women fell on their backs, which was fine, except they pulled me down to the ground with them.

The three of us were kicking each other with our dangerously heavy skates, and I thought this was it. I'd survived many fights over the years from Chechen goats in suicide vests to an elderly burlesque dancer dressed as a crawdad. But now I was going to die half naked on the streets of New Orleans at the hands of two women on roller skates. In a weird way, it seemed a bit poetic.

"Beeeee Prepaaaaaaaaaaared!" A woman's voice cried out as a familiar scooter zipped by. Knotty Nola ran over one of the women's legs, and she smashed her bat into the other's head. "Girl Scouts rule!" she shouted as the two bulls got up and skated away.

"What happened?" Franki skated up to us.

I got to my feet and thanked Nola, who flashed a Girl Scout hand signal before roaring away.

"I didn't get the phone," I panted.

Franki nodded. "I lost her, too. But not before I saw her dump this in a garbage can." She held out Kate's phone.

I grinned. "Way to go! Any idea who it was?"

Franki shook her head as we skated to the curb and up onto the sidewalk. "We might get prints off it, but I don't know. There were about four Hand Grenades thrown in with it," she said, referring to a popular local drink, "evidenced by this sticky neon-green liquid glued to it."

I sighed. "Let's go back to Valentine and Kate. I need to put my shoes back on, ditch the robe, and get some real clothes."

"Good idea," Franki said. "I'm over this *Booty Bull* bull."

WE FOUND our way back to Valentine and Kate. They gave us our shoes, and Franki handed over Kate's semi-cleaned phone.

Franki and I ran into Trashy Diva, a boutique known for retro clothing and lingerie, and I emerged wearing a garish Mardi Gras T-shirt and bright purple-and-green shorts. It was a good thing they had bras and panties, even if they were black lace with some peekaboo parts I didn't fully understand.

"What did you find out?" Valentine asked.

I told them what Knotty Nola had said about Buddy and Tibs and the French Whorens. "And they thought I was chasing one of them named La Dauphine. Doesn't that mean French prince or something?"

Valentine nodded. "It's actually *bride* of the heir to the throne."

"She's probably the next in line to be boss of that group," Kate added.

"It doesn't matter, I suppose." I shrugged. "But Nola really didn't like Buddy and Tibs."

"The stalking thing sounds bad." Kate gave me a dubious look. "But she also thinks they're bad because they were Boy Scouts?"

"It's always a suspicious thing in *my* book," I said with a slight grin.

"How's the phone?" Franki asked Kate.

She shook her head. "It still works, but whoever took it deleted the video."

A street band started up as my cell buzzed. I pulled it out of my pocket. *Unknown number*. Normally, I would've ignored it, but something told me it might be important. Especially with the girls at my house doing whatever unspeakable thing they were up to now.

After excusing myself from the group, I stepped into a somewhat quieter alley, where two homeless men were napping. One of them looked up at me before going back to sleep.

"Merry?" the woman said. "This is Dr. Wulf."

Oh good. It was just the director of Obladi Zoo. My troop was currently helping her with a fundraiser. "Did you get a different number?" I frowned at the phone.

"Yes. My old one was eaten by...that's not important. And not why I'm calling you. The girls are here. They brought in a golden poison dart frog." There was a pause. "Why do you have a golden poison dart frog?"

"They aren't on the list of what's illegal in Iowa," I insisted. "I checked."

"No," Dr. Wulf said. "They aren't. But it is highly unusual."

"I inherited him. Rufus isn't poisonous," I assured her. "He eats local bugs, not the things in the rainforest that would normally make him poisonous."

"Yes. I figured that out when Betty carried him into my office inside her mouth. Apparently, Lauren told her they had to keep him wet." She sighed. "I think I need to take a look at our junior zookeeper curriculum."

"Is Rufus okay?" I asked. "I don't have much time. I'm standing on a very crowded street corner in New Orleans, and I need to go before the angry French Whorens find me and start beating me with foam bats."

If Dr. Wulf thought this was unusual, she didn't say so. "Oh, I see. It appears Rufus is fine."

"Good!" I was relieved. Then I thought about it. "Why did they bring him to the zoo?"

"They were worried he'd miss being around other frogs. Unfortunately, the girls let him loose in the rainforest exhibit. I'm sure we'll find him." She didn't sound that confident.

Rufus was missing? I loved that little nonverbal amphibian! He was the only one who wasn't intimidated by my fat feline, Fuhrer.

The others were waving me over to the car, indicating it was time to go.

"You don't think he's in danger or anything, do you?" I asked.

"Oh…no…" Dr. Wulf said haltingly. "As long as he doesn't get close to the caiman alligators, he should be all right."

As I hung up, a text appeared on my screen. It was a link to a website for animalfreedomrightsandanonymousfreedomfightersinWho'sThere.com. I wasn't sure, but the howler monkeys kind of had faces that looked like the girls in my troop. And there was a headline:

Rare Golden Poison Dark Frog Liberated From Dangerous Animal Smuggler—Returned To The Wild In Stunning Win For Animal Rights!

There was a picture of Rufus sitting on a banana plant leaf, wearing a tiny Che Guevara-style beret with a banner behind him that read *"Patria o Muerta! Venceremos!"*

Liberty or death! and *We shall overcome*!

And I hadn't even realized I was oppressing amphibians.

FRANKI

TRACI ANDRIGHETTI

"Me-*owww*, kitten." A thirtyish male slurping a Tropical Itch from a big red tiki cup shot me a predatory smile, purring so loud I could hear it over the blaring jazz of the street band.

The guy had some nerve catcalling like that. But in all fairness, I *was* standing outside Trashy Diva in a retro leopard Trapeze coat dress that the boutique called the "Caramel Cat." "Leopards don't meow. Now scat, or you might get skinned."

He slunk off to scratch his Tropical Itch somewhere else, which was a relief. I was too tired and sore to tussle with the guy after skating down the French Whoren who'd snatched Kate's phone, not to mention falling flat on my back in the kiddie pool at the Burgundy Bar.

Come to think of it, I could use one of those Mudbug drinks used to fuel Caressa.

"Franki!" Kate shouted. "Over here!"

I scanned the crowd that had gathered around the band, but I didn't see her or Merry or Valentine. We needed to get going because time was of the essence—not for Jim in jail, but for us. It was happy hour in the French Quarter, which meant lechers were lurking. Even Kate in her condition could land a date if she wasn't careful.

As I weaved through the lechers' den looking for the girls, a fifty-something in dirty jeans and a T-shirt that said *Born Dat Way* stumbled into my path, hiccupped, and stared at my breasts, which the belt on my coat dress overemphasized. "Tell me, gorgeoush"—his brow and the corner of his mouth shot up, down, and up again—"can a leopard loozhe its shpots so I can shee those big booshoms?"

My brow and the corner of my mouth went decisively down. "I don't know what way you were born, pal, but if you don't back off, you'll die dat way."

The music stopped, and he lurched aside.

"One thing is certain," I muttered, making my way through dispersing drunks, "it's a good thing I didn't buy one of Trashy Diva's lingerie dresses."

A man spun to face me, his forty-year-old face alight with hope—and the LED boobs on his Mardi Gras beads. "Did you say *trashy lingerie?*"

"That's it." I pulled out my phone and dialed Glenda's number. In the span of two hours, I'd gone from a Tiger Eye to a Booty Bull to a Big-Bosomed Leopard, and I was ready to return to a jeans-wearing human. Nevertheless, given the action I was getting, I planned to re-wear all of the outfits—for my fiancé, Bradley, of course.

"Perfect timing, Miss Franki," Glenda drawled into the phone. "I just won the straddle-off by a considerable spread."

I knew better than to ponder the *spread* double entendre for fear of the visual it would elicit. "Great. You can bring me my clothes."

"No can do, sugar. Buddy and Tibs haven't returned from dropping off my mother."

"What do Buddy and Tibs have to do with this?"

"They run a car service called Where Y'at Limos. How do you

think I got to the Burgundy Bar from the mansion?"

"But they weren't in the limo. They were in the bar, watching the dancing."

A click ensued, followed by a deep inhale from what had to be her cigarette holder. "I told them to go in so I could get you into your Tiger Eye costume. I had a feeling it would be ugly."

I suspected another double entendre, but for the sake of my ego, I didn't pursue the matter. At least I knew why Buddy and Tibs were at the club, but I continued to have doubts about them, especially after what Merry had learned from Nola. "Did they, by any chance, take Caressa to the Running of the Bulls?"

Glenda blew out smoke. "No, to Fleur de Tease for her evening performance."

Caressa was doing *another* show? I really had to try one of those Mudbug drinks.

"Speaking of running and bulls, Miss Franki, I need to let you go. It seems I've picked up a rather obstinate stalker."

"What?" I scanned the street for lechers. "Is it the first time this has happened?"

She gave a raucous laugh. "Lawd no, child. They're part and parcel of the adult entertainment business. My mother had so many, she installed a security camera outside the mansion. Too bad she didn't leave it when she moved out."

"Yeah. It could've helped us solve Delphine's murder."

"Now that you mention it"—Glenda took another drag— "my mother once expressed surprise that Delphine had a stalker."

"Yeah, Buddy and Tibs, from what I've heard."

"Oh, pshaw. Those old coots wouldn't harm a down-and-out dolphin."

I wasn't so sure. "Just be careful."

"That's one option, sugar. But my stalker's so smokin' hot, I'd like to explore others. *Au revoir.*"

The girls approached, and I shoved the phone into my back

pocket. "What happened to you guys? I heard Kate call me, but I didn't see you."

Merry swallowed a bite of something. "We made an emergency pit stop at a tourist shop for a box of Aunt Sally's pralines."

"Kate had a craving." Valentine used a wipe to clean what I suspected was caramelized sugar residue from her fingers.

Kate tore into a package with her teeth. "Did you know Aunt Sally's comes in different flavors?"

"Four," I said with an edge. "Creamy, bananas Foster, chocolate, and café au lait. What *else* did I miss?" I asked, hinting that I didn't get my praline, which was about to go to one of Kate's twins.

She licked her fingers, rubbing it in. "We were talking about the French Whoren who deleted the video from my phone. It might've been *her* black-gloved hand we saw steal Delphine's phone from the bar in the security footage."

"Possibly." I chewed my thumbnail in the absence of a praline. "But more than one person could be involved in the murder."

Merry nodded. "I was thinking the same thing. Concepción and her grandfather, a.k.a. the former king's cousin Eduardo, a.k.a. the Hollywood agent George."

Valentine tossed the wipe into a trashcan. "The man *is* a fraud. Plus, I thought it was odd that Concepción left the mansion without a word, especially after she'd vowed to stay until she'd found her grandmother's killer."

I turned to Merry. "Don't forget Buddy and Tibs. You said yourself that Knotty Nola told you Delphine considered having a restraining order put on them. And Glenda just told me they own Where Y'at Limos. Not only did they drive Glenda to the Burgundy Bar, they drove Caressa from the bar to Fleur de Tease to do another show."

Merry shook her head. "I'd like to have one quarter of that woman's stamina."

I'd settle for an eighth.

Kate polished off my praline. "Maybe they drove Delphine to the Burgundy Bar or the mansion this morning."

Valentine put her hands on her hips. "I say we call Where Y'at Limos and find out."

"Let's try Fleur de Tease first," I said. "It's on the next block by Jackson Square."

Everyone agreed, so I led them up Royal Street and hooked a right.

Merry gestured at a café in an old red brick building. "This is Pirate's Alley."

I glanced over my shoulder. "Yeah, it dead-ends at Jackson Square."

Valentine produced her phone and snapped a picture, chuckling that Max, her employee, would love this. "Did pirates actually hang out here, Franki?"

"Allegedly, Jean Lafitte in the early 1800's. And modern-day pirates come to swashbuckle at various local festivals like Shore Leave, NOLA Pyrate Week, and Pirates of the Pontchartrain."

She dropped her phone into her beauty bag. "Sounds like a lot of rum and debauchery."

Merry beamed. "Sounds like I need to come back for that."

"I don't know." Kate rounded her shoulders and glanced behind her. "This alley is awfully dark and narrow."

"Don't worry." My smile was reassuring. "We're far safer with pirates than we are the French Quarter lechers."

We entered Jackson Square. The small courtyard between St. Louis Cathedral and the wrought-iron-fenced park with an equestrian statue of then General Andrew Jackson was a hotspot for tourists, artists, and tarot card readers. Across the street, Washington Artillery Park served as an overlook for the Mississippi River.

Kate pointed to a tour guide holding a Haunted History sign. "When we get Jim out of jail, we should all take their ghost and vampire tour."

126

A chill ran through my veins. "Count me out. A couple of years ago, I investigated the murder of a frat boy who went on one of those tours, and I discovered New Orleans has an entire community of people who live as vampires."

"Hmm." Kate gazed at the *Creole Queen* paddle-wheeler docked in the distance. "Maybe a jazz dinner cruise."

After my experience investigating a homicide on the Steamboat *Galliano*, we were better off with the vampires.

Valentine tapped my arm. "Look at that mime pretending to sleep standing up."

I looked at the shabbily dressed man leaning against the fence. "That's not a mime. It's Ray, a local drunk sleeping off a bender. He's got a bad back, so he naps on his feet."

Kate gazed at the paintings displayed on the fence. "I would love to have one of the artists paint Laurie's portrait."

"If you're going over there," Valentine said, shading her eyes, "I'd like a quick peek inside those darling boutiques."

Merry glanced at her phone and then eyed a tarot card reader. "I've got an amphibian issue to attend to."

Maybe it was the name of my dress, but the phrase "like herding cats" came to mind. On the other hand, they *had* come to The Big Easy for a vacation, and it wasn't like Jim was going anywhere. "Okay. Meet back here in twenty minutes."

The girls scattered, and I headed for Fleur de Tease on Chartres Street. I spotted the limo parked near Muriel's restaurant. Perfect! Exactly what I'd been hoping to find. Buddy stood outside the driver's side door doing a sleeping Ray impersonation, and Tibs snored in the front passenger seat.

Quietly, I opened a back door and climbed inside. My clothes were on the bar next to a half-empty champagne bottle. I lay on the floor, pulled on my jeans under my dress, and slipped my shirt around my neck. As I wriggled out of the Caramel Cat, I kicked something and sat up.

A phone!

In a dolphin-themed case.

"Is it?" I whispered. I picked it up with a bar napkin and tapped the power button. An old picture appeared on the display of Delphine with the former king's cousin.

I finished dressing and leaned into the front seat. "Wake up!"

Tibs jumped and spun around in his seat.

Buddy threw open the door. "How the hell did you get in here?"

"Never mind that." I held up the phone. "This belongs to Delphine, and I found it on the floor of your limousine. Did you drive her to the mansion today?"

Buddy's eyes popped. "No. I don't know how that got in here."

"Me neither," Tibs said.

"Really?" I caught sight of my raised brow in the rearview mirror and realized my cat-eye liner had really accentuated the Caramel Cat dress. "Because Knotty Nola said Delphine considered taking out a restraining order against you."

Tibs rolled his eyes. "Knotty Nola is a nut."

Buddy slid behind the wheel. "And Delphine was a drunk who lost touch with reality a long time ago. We were fans. That's it. She just misunderstood our intentions."

"Besides…" Tibs rubbed his nose, "a lot of men were obsessed with Delphine. That dolphin costume was sexy."

"I'll say." Buddy winked at his friend. "It had a blowhole."

The two men exchanged a lascivious grin.

My lips curled. One thing was clear. Buddy and Tibs were freaky Flipperophiles. "None of this explains how Delphine's phone got into your limo. Where were the two of you when she was killed?"

Tibs glanced at Buddy. "Driving a group from an OBGYN convention to The Penthouse strip club in Baton Rouge."

Buddy grabbed a pen and a business card. "I'll give you their number. You can call to confirm the details."

"That won't be necessary." The police would verify their alibi, and I wanted nothing to do with male gynecologists. "Why did you go to Caressa's old mansion this morning?"

"To apologize." Buddy tossed the pen on the dashboard. "She'd called for a ride to the Burgundy Bar, but we'd already booked the OBGYNs."

Tibs ran a hand through his thinning hair. "We drove straight from Baton Rouge to her mansion. She didn't tell us she'd sold the place to Glenda."

I stared from one to the other. "This morning you said you lived down the street from the mansion, so if you'd just returned from that driving gig, why were you *walking* by instead of driving?"

Buddy shrugged. "We parked in our driveway and gave our knees a rest. Driving limo is murder on the arthritis."

I decided to give them a break and instead concentrated on the reference to my ex-stripper landlady. Suddenly a terrible thought struck me. But it couldn't be. "Who else have you given rides to today?"

Tibs looked at Buddy, who was visibly concerned. "Besides the OBGYNs…" Tibs rubbed his chin, "just Glenda and Caressa earlier."

I grabbed the champagne bottle and took a slug. Caressa had an alibi for the time of Delphine's murder.

But did Glenda?

"Francesca Lucia Amato," I chided, imitating my mother as I headed for Jackson Square to meet Merry, Kate, and Valentine. "There is no way Glenda had Delphine's phone, much less murdered her. That phone was stolen from the Burgundy Bar before Glenda came to the mansion."

A realization made my feet as heavy as my heart, and I stopped dead on Chartres Street. I didn't know where my ex-stripper landlady had been before she came to meet us at her house.

Did Glenda take Delphine's phone from the bar and then follow her to the mansion, where she killed her?

"Not a chance." I shook my head and resumed walking. I had a hard time believing Glenda was a killer, but she *was* fiercely competitive. Even though she'd retired from stripping, she hadn't given up competitions. Case in point—the straddle-off at the Burgundy Bar. Not only that. She'd recently won Pole-A-Palooza in Indiana and Pirates of the Caribooty in Oregon.

My feet skidded to a halt. "Oh God."

Did Glenda kill Delphine over some competition like the straddle-off? At the age of ninety, I couldn't imagine Delphine had much spread. Or were Glenda and her mother collaborating on the murder? Caressa could've taken the phone from the bar, seen something she didn't like, and had Glenda kill Delphine.

"Ugh." I pressed my fingertips to my lips. "Franki, what's wrong with you?"

"That's what *I* was wondering," a woman said from the side of her mouth as she speed-walked past me.

"That was uncalled for," I shouted. "I'm having a completely sane personal crisis."

The woman continued walking without a care for my well-being. The only thing to do was follow Merry's lead and talk to a tarot card reader.

When I entered Jackson Square, I saw Merry, Kate, and Valentine on kiddie stools around a low table I didn't dare approach.

It belonged to Mama Esther. Instead of tarot, she read bones that looked like phalanges from human fingers. No matter what I said or did, the uppity bone-thrower had a bone to pick with me.

Mama Esther's brown eyes made contact with mine, her eye sockets bulging. "Are you ladies with *her*?"

Merry turned to me. "Yeah, she lives here. We came to visit."

Mama Esther blew a breath from her chubby cheeks and

covered her bones with a conch shell. "Then y'all gonna need more help than I can give ya."

Kate leaned forward and squeezed Mama Esther's hand. "*Please*. My husband, Jim, was arrested for the murder we told you about."

Another sigh escaped Mama Esther's lips. "I'll try for those unborn babies." She tightened the knot on her headscarf. "But I cain't promise you nuthin'. *Dat one's* a head case."

One of these days I should knot that headscarf around her—

My phone rang, and the number made my blood run colder than New Orleans vampires. My mother was calling from my parents' house in Houston, which meant my nonna would be on the line. Better their meddling than Mama Esther's mouth. I tapped Answer. "Hi, Mom."

"Franki," my nonna rasped, "we saw you on-a the five-o-clock-a news."

The declaration was not unlike a blow from a RollerBull's bat. Did someone film me in my Tiger Eye costume at the Burgundy Bar? "Um, what was I doing?"

"You were skating, Francesca." My mom's tone was as dry as the finger bones on Mama Esther's table. "In a risqué gown that showed your *culo*."

Relief flooded my chest, and I sank onto a public bench that faced St. Louis Cathedral. My mom would've been outraged at me mud-wrestling in a burlesque club, and my nonna would've been outraged at the tips I didn't get.

"Did-a that-a booty robe get-a you some dates?"

My nonna, like my mother, was well aware that I was engaged to Bradley, but neither of them would stop until I had a wedding ring on my finger and a focaccia in the oven. "The bulls were women, Nonna. Roller Girls. I spent the whole time fending off their advances."

"Women?" Nonna spat. "Then-a how the hell-a are we gonna get a *bambino*?"

That was a conversation for another day, i.e., when inferno froze over. "I'm investigating a case. Delphine the Dolphin Girl was murdered this morning."

"Mamma mia!"

I lurched upright on the bench. "Did you know her, Nonna?"

"No, I'm just-a shock-ed she was-a still alive."

This from a woman who was eighty-two.

"Carmela," my mother shrilled, "wasn't Delphine's father Sicilian?"

"Sure. When-a your nonnu, God rest-a his soul, and I lived in-a New Orleans, Delphine's-a father, Delfino, used-a to buy our produce. He was a *gran bugiardo*."

I ignored the fact that she'd called him a "huge liar" to contemplate his name. A man called "Dolphin" was weird but not uncommon in Italy.

"Delfino used-a to brag-a that his-a ancestor was-a the girl in-a the *Teste di Moro* legend."

My mother cleared her throat. "She's talking about the Moor's Head tradition, Francesca. You know the story."

All too well. A Sicilian girl found out her Moorish boyfriend had a wife and children, so she cut off his head and made a vase out of it as one does when she's been betrayed. "It's a hard story to forget."

"And-a so is-a the moral. Never betray a *siciliana*."

"First of all, Nonna, that's a stereotype, so you shouldn't say it."

"*What* a stereotype?" she cried. "Delphine was-a almost a hundred years-a old! Back then, the legend was-a told-a to us like a fairy tale."

And it was even more grim than the Brothers Grimm. "I'm sorry, Nonna. I don't see what the vase story has to do with Delphine's murder. If she was out for revenge against her killer, she didn't get it."

"Well," my mother sing-songed, "Delphine *was* only half Sicilian, dear."

"And-a mark-a my words, she was-a out for vendetta."

The clock on St. Louis Cathedral tolled. It was five-thirty, so the girls and I had to move. "It's getting late, and I just found Delphine's phone in a place it shouldn't have been."

"Franki." Nonna had turned on the pleading voice she used to convince priests to pray for my continued fertility. "Listen to your nonna. Don't-a spend-a too much-a time on-a that investigation. Delphine was about-a to kick-a the bucket, anyway."

"*Carmela*," my mother protested. Feebly.

I crossed myself, which seemed particularly necessary since I was in the presence of a Catholic church.

"What-a, Brenda?" Nonna snapped at my mother. "It's-a the weekend! Franki needs-a to have-a some fun! I checked the convention schedule, and-a the State-a and Local Benefits Association is in-a town. There's-a lots of-a men."

I hung up. The OBGYN convention was appealing by comparison.

Valentine took a seat next to me. "Did we hear you correctly? You found Delphine's phone?"

"Yeah." I sighed. "Either Caressa or Glenda dropped it in the limo."

"Glenda?" Kate collapsed in the more-than-reasonable space beside me, knocking me into Valentine.

Merry avoided the seating issue by leaning over the back of the bench on her forearms. "We've got to crack the password."

I used the bar nap to pull the phone from my bag. "But our fingerprints will be on it."

She waved off my reluctance. "Yeah, but Valentine and I have the hair show alibi."

Valentine pulled a box of what looked like ClingWrap from her beauty bag. "I've got just the thing. Haircoloring film I brought for the show."

"Perfect." I wrapped my left hand and right index finger, marveling at her ability to turn hair products into sleuthing tools. "Okay, the password has to be six numbers or letters or both."

Merry studied the ground. "That rules out 'Delphine,' 'dolphin,' 'burlesque,' 'Caressa,' and 'Concepción.' How about 'George?' Or 'cousin?'"

Holding my breath, I tried both and threw in "Glenda." I exhaled so hard my cheeks puffed like Mama Esther's. "Nope."

"Try her birthday," Kate said. "It's probably on Wikipedia.

A Google search produced June thirtieth. "It's not the password, but ironically she's a water sign."

Kate massaged her belly. "Try 'Cancer.'"

Valentine nodded. "And 'dancer.'"

Merry pursed her lips and looked at me. "1800OLDSLUT? No, that's a phone number. Sorry."

I tried Kate and Valentine's suggestions with no luck. "We might need to get David and The Vassal on this. They're computer science majors at Tulane, so they're experts at cracking passwords."

Mama Esther aimed her wry gaze at the girls. "What's a six-character synonym for *Karen*?"

"I am not a *Karen*," I huffed. "Why don't you help by throwing those bones instead of pointing fingers?" I glanced at the bones. "Uh, *metaphorical* fingers."

Mama Esther's brows disappeared behind her headscarf. "Mmm-*hmm*. Angry *and* obstinate, two of the Karen qualities."

I didn't reply. Her snarky jab reminded me of what my nonna had said about Delphine being half Sicilian. *Revenge*, *vendetta*, and *buttana*, the Sicilian word for *whore*, were too many letters. "Wait. Concepción said Delphine called Caressa a 'Jezebel harlot.'"

Merry raised her hands and looked around for support. "That's basically what I said."

"Wait a minute." Valentine leaned in, her flowery perfume

filling my nostrils. "Why would Delphine use a password on *her* phone that described *Caressa*?"

"Good point." I chewed my lip. "Although, if you believe my nonna, Delphine had vendetta-against-Caressa on the brain."

Valentine gave an *okay then* shrug, which shed another stray feather from her outfit, then watched with the others as I tried *harlot*.

The display cleared. "We're in."

I scrolled through phone calls and checked for email addresses. Within minutes, I'd found a phone call that coincided with an audio recording. "From today at 8:31 a.m."

Kate clutched my arm with the strength of three people. "That's right before Delphine and Caressa faced off in the Burgundy Bar security footage."

I shook some feeling back in my arm before pushing Play. Would the audio recording incriminate Glenda? I pressed my lips tight, hesitating. But if it did, at least I'd finally have an excuse to move out of that dump of an apartment she rented to me.

The thud of bones hitting the table made us all spin.

Four bones rolled to the ground. As if they were indeed phalanges from human fingers, one each pointed at us sleuths.

Mama Esther wailed, "Erzulie D'en Tort!"

Her eyes rolled back, but she lurched forward.

Before we could react, Mama Esther slid from her kiddie stool and face-planted among the bones.

AUDIO RECORDING FROM DELPHINE'S CELL PHONE

LESLIE LANGTRY

8:31 a.m.

DELPHINE

…and then I'll be famous! I'll be even richer!

CONCEPCIÓN

I heard some strange sound just now. You're not…are you recording this conversation?

DELPHINE

No, I'm *un*-recording it.

CONCEPCIÓN

That's not a thing. Wait, were you recording it before now?

DELPHINE

Don't be an idiot! I don't know how to record phone calls, just how to *un*-record them.

CONCEPCIÓN

That doesn't make sense.

DELPHINE

Anyway, like I was saying…gin is two for one at the liquor store, so I thought I'd get about ten bottles and about thirty limes…

CONCEPCIÓN

That's not what you were talking about. You were telling me you're going to Caressa's to steal something out of that pearl that'll launch you into the big time.

DELPHINE

I was? Oh. That sounds important. Well, if I'm gonna be rich, I should visit the bank and move around my money.

CONCEPCIÓN

How much do you have to move? Don't you think I should help you with your finances?

DELPHINE

No. A lot. Wait. That didn't come out right. A lot, and no. That's what I meant.

Pause

I'm sure I said it right the first time. You just asked your questions out of order.

CONCEPCIÓN

Don't you think Eduardo and I should be helping you manage your wealth? Isn't it time you made me your executor? At least grant me financial power of attorney. I have the papers made up and can run them by.

DELPHINE

Suspiciously

Why all the questions? Why are you badgering me?

CONCEPCIÓN

I'm not badgering you, *Abuelita*. I'm just concerned for your well-being. I'd hate to see you make a mistake that might leave me...I mean, *you* with no money.

DELPHINE

You want my money!

CONCEPCIÓN

You're reading too much into this. I'm your only heir, and I asked a couple of *very* innocent and *totally* normal questions.

DELPHINE

Shouting

Oh no you don't! You don't get to find out about my money! That's what you're really after! You're always asking about power of attorney and wanting to have me psychiatrically evaluated.

CONCEPCIÓN

Snaps

You sound like a demented old woman! I'm your granddaughter! I care about you!

DELPHINE

No you don't! You just want me dead so you can inherit my fortune!

CONCEPCIÓN

You have a fortune?

Laughs

See? I care so little about money I didn't even know about that!

DELPHINE

You did too. You always were a little schemer! And I'm not telling you nothing!

CONCEPCIÓN

Let's just calm down. You're overreacting. I'm afraid you're going to have a heart attack.

DELPHINE mutters something under her breath.

What did you say? I didn't catch that.

DELPHINE

Oh. I forgot I was still on the phone.

CONCEPCIÓN

See? Right there! Eduardo's concerned about you, too, and now you just proved that you need my help!

DELPHINE

No! I know what you're up to! You and Eduardo are in cahoots! And I'm going to expose you both!

CONCEPCIÓN

Snarling

Demented and crazy. That's what you are.

DELPHINE

Yeah, well you know what else I am? Smart enough to go see my lawyer to change my will. That happens today!

Silence on the line.

CONCEPCIÓN

I'm coming over. You're completely unstable and shouldn't be alone.

Noise in the background of a blender running.

Abuelita? Are you there?

DELPHINE

Singing

Gin is a sin...there's so much sin in gin.

Pause

Wait...maybe it's *there is no sin in gin.* I need to find that lyric sheet. I think it's in my thong drawer.

CONCEPCIÓN

You have to hang up the phone! I should take that away from you. Hello?

DELPHINE

Oh, hello. Is this Antoine's? Do you deliver? I'd like an order of Oysters Rockefeller. Can you grub them on the hub?

CONCEPCIÓN

Growling

That's it, old woman. I'm coming over. And you're going to a psych ward, or I'm going to kill you!

DELPHINE

Suck it, Concepción!

Blender roars to life.

Call ends.

VALENTINE

ARLENE MCFARLANE

This whole thing was creeping me out. Mama Esther's loud cry was the cherry on top. What had we gotten involved in? Murdered burlesque dancers? Vicious roller derby bulls? Now an eccentric bone thrower? I thought my hometown, Rueland, Massachusetts, had problems. Granted, Rueland did have its share of crazies, but New Orleans took the cake...*and* the cherry on top.

I didn't waste another second reflecting on everything that had gone wrong since I'd met up with my friends. There was a very large woman down, and she was going to need help coming to and getting to her feet.

I rummaged through my bag until I found my small can of facial mister. Normally, the ionic mist was used to moisturize the epidermis, and at the moment Mama Esther's skin was already drenched in sweat, but without rousing her with a gallon of water, this was the next best thing.

I sprayed the fine mist an inch from her nose, and she opened her big round eyes and sneezed.

"Lawd thunderin', child! What'd you do dat for?"

I slid the can back in my bag, and Merry and I helped her to her feet.

"You passed out. Remember?"

She slid a watchful eye toward Franki, then harrumphed. "I remember dat my bones don't lie. And you four best be careful because Erzulie D'en Tort is angry. Now be on your way. I want nuthin' to do with the lot of you."

That was fine by me. I had no intention of hanging around where I wasn't wanted. On top of which, I wasn't going to argue with someone of Mama Esther's nature. She'd obviously seen something in the bones that lay scattered, facing the four of us, and spooky territory wasn't my thing.

"You heard the lady," I said, my upbeat voice belying the nervousness I felt inside. "Let's get out of Dodge before someone needles us with...with a *voodoo doll.*"

"*Aaaaah!*" Mama Esther shrieked at my words, swiftly lifting one of the hems from her flowing, layered dress to fan herself.

Franki glanced around, then covered her mouth with her hand and hushed her voice. "We better avoid the voodoo references. Mama Esther said Erzulie d'en Tort is already angry, and on the off chance that voodoo *loas* are real, we don't want to make her any madder. Her name means 'Erzulie of the Wrongs' because she deals revenge to those who've wronged women and children."

"Why would this Erzulie be mad at us?" I asked.

"Yeah," Merry said. "We didn't *wrong* anyone."

Franki shrugged. "The bone throw seems to indicate otherwise, but Mama Esther could just be a lousy shot."

Mama Esther raised a brow and a bone. "Wanna try me?"

Kate shivered. "Let's get out of here."

"Not before we listen to this audio recording." Franki held up Delphine's phone and shot a defiant glare at Mama Esther, looking as brave as Scarlett O'Hara in that famous, gritty, crimson-night scene in *Gone With the Wind*, when she raised her fist vowing she'd never go hungry again.

"Yeah," Kate agreed. "Maybe there's something there that will vindicate Jim."

"Shoo, shoo!" Mama Esther waved us away. "Go do dat somewhere else."

We shuffled further away from Mama Esther and the crowd and closer to St. Louis Cathedral, which, blessedly, made me feel a smidgen safer from the voodoo vibe in the street.

Franki brought up the recording, and we huddled together, heads close to the phone, trying to make sense of the conversation between Delphine and Concepción.

"Listen to that girl disrespecting her grandma," Kate said, hands on her abundant hips. "If Laurie ever talked to me like that, I'd...I'd...well, I don't know what I'd do, but she sure wouldn't get away with it."

Merry slid Kate a smile, then shook her head, her fading blue curls springing in every direction. "Concepción is a sly one, all but demanding that Delphine hand over her fortune."

"Hand over...her fortune." I ruminated on Merry's comment while putting the puzzle pieces together. "That's it! La Dauphine, who those rough French Whorens thought you were chasing. They were talking about Concepción!"

"Of course!" Franki slapped her leg. "Who else would care so much about deleting anything from Kate's phone?"

"Yeah..." Kate hesitated, "but that means she would've known I recorded the footage from the bar."

"It's possible," I added. "After all, one minute she was at the mansion, and the next she was at the Burgundy Bar. Maybe she heard us talking about going there and wanted to keep an eye on us."

I focused on Kate. "And you *had* mentioned she bustled into the dressing room when you were changing out of your green satin outfit, remember?"

Kate fanned her face from the heat. "Oh gosh, yes. I have pregnancy brain. But you're right. She strutted into the dressing room, on her phone, exclaiming, 'It's gone!' And 'Now what do we do?'"

"She obviously knows more than what she's been telling us," I said. "And I don't know how much stock I'd put into what she *has* been telling us."

Kate bobbed her head up and down. "The more I think about it, she could've been lurking around the bar after that dressing-room exchange, spying on me, on all of us."

Franki tsked several times. "Looks like my nonna was right."

"About what?" Merry asked.

After hearing Franki's nonna's story that Delphine's father had been known as a huge liar back in the day, we were all likely thinking the same thing—the apple didn't fall far from the tree.

I stared down at Delphine's phone in Franki's palm. "Seems Concepción came by her boldness and lying personality honestly."

Who was I to talk? Hadn't we all told a fib now and then? But to use an old woman like this in hopes of gaining an inheritance? And to threaten her as Concepción did? I shivered inwardly. That type of behavior took cold calculation.

"To make matters worse," I said, "Eduardo, a.k.a. George, a.k.a. a dozen other names—who by the way is a terrible flirt—told me he'd be coming into some money soon, and would I want to flee to the Riviera with him and bask naked in the sun on a nude beach."

Merry wrinkled up her nose. "The guy's old enough to be your grandfather."

"Don't remind me. I can't get the naked beach visuals out of my head."

"If Delphine was right," Franki said, "and Concepción and Eduardo were in cahoots, then we know the guy's up to no good. This audio recording confirms it."

"Maybe the real reason he came to town was to off Delphine," I concluded.

"Agreed." Kate slid onto another nearby bench. "We already know Concepción was the roller girl who stole my phone. Now what?"

Merry tapped her foot on the ground while she thought, and Franki narrowed her eyes on the cathedral—maybe for divine intervention. I glanced from the three of them to a red-and-black figure in the background.

"I don't know, but I think I just saw our prime suspect slip into that public bathroom. Let me see if I can find answers." I tightened my bag under my arm and hurried across the street.

I wasn't feeling especially brave, knowing I was about to confront the tough-as-nails Concepción, but I wasn't going to sit back either. She held the key to this mystery, and the inquisitive side of me needed to find out what she was hiding.

I stepped into the cool, concrete-walled bathroom as a small child finished washing her hands and ran back out into the hot sunshine. I took a deep breath, thinking I could stay in here all day if it meant escaping the humid heat. But I had a job to do, and as my target was here and we were alone, I needed to act fast.

Concepción had her phone in hand and looked as though she were mid-dial.

Hmm. Who was she calling? Eduardo, her partner-in-crime? Her lawyer?

She spotted me and promptly stuffed her phone inside her black spandex shorts, then faced the mirror and made a show of primping her long black hair.

I approached the sink and moistened my hands and wrists in an effort to cool off, all the while avoiding eye contact with Concepción.

I could tell she was sizing me up in the mirror, and a beat later she turned to me, her Spanish accent rich, her voice sultry. "How do you keep your hair so glossy?"

Her question surprised me, considering her hair had its own vibrant shine. I could've gone into a long explanation of my background in the beauty industry, disclosing the products I use and my easy daily routine, but I shrugged lightheartedly, deciding simple was best. "Good genes, I guess."

"Ha!" she barked out a laugh. "The only genes *I* inherited were ghastly."

Play dumb, I thought. "Ghastly?"

"You don't want to know." She gaped down at herself. "Look at me in this stupid-o outfit, all for the sake of—" She rambled off a few sentences in Spanish, arms waving, feet stomping, getting more worked up by the minute, then suddenly realized who she was talking to. "Oh, darn. You didn't understand any of that...did you?"

Had she just spilled the beans, or perhaps confessed, and I'd missed it?

"Uh, no. Now if you'd spoken French I would've had something to say back."

She eyed me warily. "I like you, *chica bonita*. You're different from the others." She gave me a thorough once-over, choosing her words carefully. "You appreciate fashion, you're full of style, and you exude warmth."

I didn't know if she was trying to flatter me or if this was leading up to something, but I was willing to play nice. "How long have you been a roller derby girl?"

She tugged at the hem of her red shirt. "Where I come from, we start on roller skates at a young age. It's like...how you say, second nature."

Didn't really answer my question, but I nodded thoughtfully, buying time. "And why did you steal Kate's phone?"

So much for playing dumb.

She laughed in my face. "Me? Steal that tubby *madrecita's* phone? Why would I do a thing like that?"

I trilled out a fake laugh along with her, then pounced, my

145

stern look showing I didn't appreciate her criticism. "First, Kate is not tubby. She's *pregnant*. There's a difference."

"*Pff.*" She waved me away like a fly.

"And secondly, you stole her phone so you could see if there was anything incriminating on it. In fact, there's a good possibility there's more to all this than removing Kate's data."

"You don't know what you're talking about." She swept her hair around her shoulder and pierced a sharp, brown-eyed glare at me.

"I think I do, and I'll bet if we talk to Louis Armstrong he'll share what you confided in him earlier today." I actually wasn't betting on this. No lawyer worth his salt would betray a client's trust, but Concepción needed to know we were onto her.

"Rubbish!" she erupted. "That scrawny, two-bit lawyer wouldn't know his head from his *culo*! And none of this matters because Louis has given up the case...and he's giving up on Jim. You can take *that* back to that household drudge he's married to and the rest of your meddling, *amigas locas*."

Blood pounded in my temples, and I ground my teeth. Spanish wasn't my mother tongue like it was for my Argentinean employee, Jock, but I did know *loco* meant crazy. I even knew that Concepción was using the feminine version of the word because she was referring to four female friends.

I'd slipped my hand in my bag and was clenching a bottle of perm solution. I'd once squirted it into a felon's face, and I was close to spraying it at Concepción to bring her down a notch for insulting my friends.

Calm down, Valentine. Fighting fire with fire won't help. I wasn't so sure about this, but I took a deep breath, loosened my grip on the bottle, and took the high road. "You seem to know a lot about Louis and who he's representing."

"You bet I do. One thing you can count on...Jim's going to rot in that stinky jail."

She studied me, waiting for a reaction, but I put on my world-class poker face, refusing to give her what she wanted.

"I don't think so," I said simply, showing more confidence than I felt because, in all honesty, with every passing hour I was less sure about our ability to save the day...and Jim.

"We'll see!" She flounced to the door and whipped around, a smug look on her face. "The cops have something on the guy. In other words, *chica bonita*, your *Jim* has been charged with first degree murder."

"I NEED SOME ADVICE." I leaned my hot back against the cool bathroom wall near the entrance, phone to my ear.

Romero's sigh came through the wire loud and clear. "Oh boy. What've you gotten yourself into now?"

My sigh came out louder than his, and I was beginning to regret dialing his number. "Look, I wasn't the one who found this corpse, okay?"

"That makes me feel so much better. Let me grab a beer and put my feet up now that I can relax."

Wiseacre.

"And since you haven't found any corpses," he went on, "you'll be flying home as scheduled, correct?"

"Uh...not exactly."

By the growing silence, I could tell his frustration was building. "Which brings me back to my original question. What've you gotten yourself into now?"

I felt a pang in my chest but put it aside while I organized my thoughts. Then I gave Romero the highlights since I'd arrived in New Orleans, concluding with Concepción's huffy exit from the bathroom.

After I finished, I realized the pang in my heart wasn't for poor

Jim or Kate or even the dear departed Delphine. Truth was, I missed this strong, dangerously sexy, hard-headed yet surprisingly sensitive detective who always smelled enticingly of Arctic Spruce cologne.

"Wait…" His deep, husky chuckle told me he found this all amusing. "You performed on stage in a *burlesque bar?*"

Leave it to Romero to focus on the sexy part. "As I *said*, I was trying to get information on Caressa."

"A ninety-something-year-old burlesque dancer," he stated as if clarifying this for himself. "Hold on a minute while I wipe that image from my mind."

"I know it sounds ludicrous, but burlesque dancing is a big thing down here…no matter what the age."

"Apparently. And another aged dancer got the hook, so to speak."

"Yes, Delphine the Dolphin Girl."

"You're not making this stuff up, are you." He said this in an affirmative manner, his tone level, yet I could visualize him rubbing his five-o'clock shadow in doubt.

"It's all true. And now that we've located Delphine's phone, I have a question."

"Sweetheart, you always have a question. Go ahead. Shoot. What do you want to know?"

I overlooked his sarcasm and exhaled long and slow. "This is all hypothetical, but after Concepción stormed out of the bathroom, I started thinking ahead."

"I'm following."

"I'm a bit anxious about this phone. I mean, what if something happens to it while we have it in our possession?"

"This phone, meaning Delphine's, not Kate's."

"Correct. Keep up."

He sighed. "Lord knows I'm trying." He must've been mulling this over. He was quiet for a beat, then said, "You *are* going to turn it over to the police…right?"

"Right." Eventually.

"Then what's the problem?"

I blew out air, feeling myself getting worked up. "Let's say Concepción got her hands on Delphine's phone as she insisted she would in the audio recording."

"The phone which is in your possession."

I grimaced, realizing I hadn't clarified that part. "It's actually in Franki's possession."

"Of course." He probably added an eye roll to that.

"Then suppose Concepción deleted that incriminating conversation between her and her grandmother. Would any of our suspicions that she was involved in Delphine's murder hold up in court? With that convicting phone proof gone, it seems it'd be her word against ours."

"If there's no proof," he said, "then we'd rely on witnesses." He paused. "Are there any of those?"

I rolled my innocent gaze to the ceiling. "Um...possibly? I mean, if this hypothetical occurrence actually happened, and she *did* get her hands on Delphine's phone, there *might* be witnesses to prove what she'd done."

"Naturally. Well, I have a *real* case here back home with *actual* witnesses, so if you need any more hypothetical answers, you know where I am."

Arrogant, tough...gorgeous, irresistible cop!

I hung up and hustled back to where I'd left the others, a dozen questions whirling in my head. I shared what I'd learned from Concepción, then tapped my chin pointedly at the things that weren't adding up.

"It doesn't make sense." I focused on Franki. "Ever since you'd mentioned that Glenda or Caressa dropped the phone in the limo, it's been playing on my mind."

Everyone stared at me.

"Think about it. Caressa was arguing with Delphine in that video footage when a hand came up on the bar and stole the phone. That pretty well eliminates Caressa as a suspect. As far as

Glenda is concerned, Franki, you texted her after Delphine's body was discovered at the mansion, and she showed up a few minutes later. But do you know where she was when you texted her? I mean, could she really have been at the bar miles away, stolen Delphine's phone, and appeared at the mansion so quickly?"

Franki chewed on her lip, eyes narrowed as if she were mentally sorting things out.

I slid my bag to the ground, my stare still on her. "On top of that, what's your gut instinct say? Glenda's your landlord. Do you think she's capable of murder?"

"Ha!" she blurted. "Glenda's capable of a lot of things, most of them without clothes on."

Merry shut her eyes tightly. "Please. I'm still having bad visuals of Rufus sitting on a banana plant leaf, wearing a tiny Che Guevara-style beret on his little frog head. I don't want to picture your landlady without clothes."

I looked around the square, making sure our talk was not being overheard by anyone. All the same, I lowered my voice. "I think we need to rewind to what we saw last in regard to Caressa, Delphine, and Delphine's phone. And since it was her phone that was stolen and Delphine was soon found dead, that leaves Caressa."

Franki nodded, studying the three of us. "I believe I was the last to see Caressa, and that was in the dressing room after our mud-wrestle. But there was no phone in sight. Then Arthur, the stagehand, came in and carried her out."

"To go where?" Merry asked.

"To take her to her next act. According to Glenda, Caressa had an evening performance booked at Fleur de Tease."

I looked from one to the other as everyone processed this. Due to my impulsive nature I was beyond processing and was already squashing the unease climbing my spine.

"I think we need to talk to Arthur," I finally said.

Kate gasped. "First, can we go to the police station? I'm worried sick about Jim. I need to see that he's okay."

Now that her belly was full, Kate was in total mama mode.

"That Spanish witch is probably lying about Jim," Franki said. "Why don't you try calling the police station. Maybe you'll get some real answers."

"I did. They keep giving me the brushoff." Kate's cheeks reddened, showing her frustration. Either that or it was a pregnant flush.

"Everyone in agreement?" Franki asked. "We go check on Jim?"

"The police station it is!" Merry said.

I handed Franki a baggie to drop Delphine's phone in so she could ditch the haircoloring film from her hands. Then I shoved Ariel in another baggie to keep her from jostling around in my overloaded sack.

I gulped back a swallow and followed in step behind the others, heels clicking softly on the pavement. I didn't know what we'd discover at the police station, and I didn't know what state Jim would be in, but one thing I did know, I couldn't get Arthur out of my mind.

KATE

DIANA ORGAIN

 o Do

1. Get Jim out of jail. STAT!!
2. ☑ ~~Call mom and check in on Laurie...ugh, first get my phone back.~~ (Done)
3. ☑ ~~Figure out who this Eduardo guy really is.~~ (Done)
4. ☑ ~~Feed the twins. (Again, really?)~~ (Done)
5. ~~Ride a steamboat.~~ (Franki says the steamboat here can be problematic.)
6. Take the haunted ghost, voodoo, and vampire tour. (Will there even be time for this?)
7. Romantic dinner with Jim tonight. (No matter what!)
8. Buy souvenirs.

The four of us walked to where Franki had parked her cherry-red Mustang convertible. Truth be told, they walked, I waddled.

Merry graciously held open the front passenger side door for me. "Here *you* go, mama," she said cheerfully. "Your turn to sit in the front!"

I climbed in and tried to ignore the misery swirling in my brain. As I went to strap the seatbelt I stopped short. *"What!"*

Franki turned the key in the ignition. *"What* what?"

I burst into tears.

"Oh no! Kate! What is it?" Valentine leaned forward from the backseat and placed a cool hand on my shoulder.

"The seatbelt doesn't fit," I sputtered.

How stupid I sound!

It wasn't the seatbelt, but it was. It was everything. Jim in jail, the twins growing seemingly two inches in two hours, the heat!

"I'm ruining your vacation," I said. "I'm too big for the car, my husband's in jail, I can't do anything fun without a dead body popping up!"

"I know that feeling," Merry muttered.

A silver Tesla honked at us, impatient for the parking spot.

Franki waved a hand and shouted, "Hold the horn, pal. We're not done here yet."

"I mean, I didn't even eat that much since we were in the car last! How can the seatbelt not fit? What did I eat?"

"Everyth—" Franki stopped herself. "I mean, everything in this car sticks. Try that belt again."

My eyes stung with tears, but I nodded. I gripped the belt and lopped it over my lap. I stared in horror as it failed to reach the other side. The silence in the car was deafening, these ladies too polite to comment.

"I'm so fat!" I wailed.

"Stop it. You have two humans in there!" Franki reached over and yanked the seatbelt.

I jolted back, and Franki easily slid the belt under my belly and secured it.

Under the belly. Duh.

The Tesla gave a long loud honk.

"Stronzo," Franki muttered.

Valentine reassuringly squeezed my shoulder, while Franki revved the engine and vacated the parking spot.

I wiped my tears. "I really appreciate you all."

Merry patted my head from behind. "Don't stress, mama. We're going to figure this thing out. As for ruining my vacation. No. Absolutely not. Mud-wrestling, running with the bulls, chasing down the bad guy. Come on. We live for this kind of thing."

Franki maneuvered in and out of traffic, and before I knew it we were at the police station.

"Wait! I can't see Jim like this! He'll know I've been crying!" I pressed my hands to my face. "I'm sure I'm all red and puffy."

"I've got just the thing for you." Valentine dug into her cosmetic bag and pulled out a Gua Sha. "These little beauties are great for massaging the scalp and improving blood flow to the hair roots, but they also work on reducing puffiness in the face."

She handed me the cool jade tool, and I swept it across my face, pushing all the puffiness out from under my eyes toward my ears. I inhaled and tried to relax.

After a few minutes, my shoulders dropped and I felt the tension lift from my body. I pulled down the sun visor and peeked at my reflection in the mirror.

Much better.

I handed the Gua Sha back to Valentine. "Thank you."

Franki exited the car, looking ready to do battle. "Let's see what that Mangiaratti has to say for himself."

I TEXTED Louis Armstrong for the fourth time. *Hey, can you PLEASE give me a status update on Jim? Heard that the police have something, and it's not looking good.* There was no way I was going to take what Concepción said about Louis dropping Jim as gospel. I needed to hear it from the horse's mouth.

"No response from Armstrong," I said to Franki as we bounded up the concrete steps to New Orleans Second District Police Station. It had a rose-colored exterior, which under different circumstances, I might've found pretty.

Franki sighed. "Let's not get ahead of ourselves. Louis goes MIA sometimes." She glanced at Merry and Valentine behind us. They both gave a nod that was meant to reassure me, but only succeeded in making me more nervous.

Franki held the door for me, and I entered the beautifully appointed station. With one wall painted teal and the other dandelion yellow, the interior looked downright cheerful. Behind the front desk sat a woman officer with ringleted hair. She held a pencil in her hand and was intent on the form before her. She gave us a stern look when we approached.

"Let me do the talking," Franki said.

I bit my lip.

"Good afternoon," Franki said, smiling. "We'd like to speak with Detective Mangiaratti."

The officer looked silently at Franki, then at each of us. Instead of answering, she used the pencil to scratch her scalp.

"Listen," I said. "My husband, Jim Conn—"

Franki pivoted, her shoulder now blocking my view of the female officer. A reminder to let her do the talking.

Why was that so hard for me?

"You an attorney?" the officer asked.

"No," Franki said. "Private investigator."

"*Pff.*" The officer didn't bother keeping the disdain out of her voice. "My brother-in-law is one of those. No desk duty, doesn't follow rules, thinks he can *demand* things. You like that?"

Before Franki could reply, Merry stepped forward. "Is Detective Mangiaratti available or not?"

The woman officer tapped the pencil on the desk. "Look, Mangiaratti is out. NOPD is short-staffed, we got a visiting

155

dignitary in town, and the Running of the Bulls is in full swing. The detective's a bit too busy to talk to a PI."

I sidestepped Merry. "Look, Jim is my husband. I'd like to see him."

"No visiting hours today," she said.

"You can't hold him without cause."

Her eyes narrowed. "Actually, we can. In Louisiana, the state has 48 hours to determine probable cause."

My phone buzzed, and I glanced at the screen.

Louis Armstrong.

I pressed on the message to read his text. *Sorry, Kate. There's been a development. We need to talk.*

We're at the police station, I fired back.

Franki and Valentine looked over my shoulder as I texted the lawyer.

Merry turned her back to the woman officer and mumbled, "We should've brought her pralines. Soften her up. On one of my previous missions, in Istanbul, I had to infiltrate the Polis. I brought baklava. It was the most stupendous thing. Crispy phyllo dough, pistachios, dripping in honey—"

I grabbed Merry's arm. *"Please.* I can't text and think about food at the same time."

Merry laughed. "Sorry."

I glanced back at my phone. The three floating dots appearing by Louis's name to indicate he was typing a message flashed, then disappeared.

"Oh, for crying out loud, Louis," Franki said. "Just call him."

I nodded, then pressed his number. Franki took my elbow and ushered me away from the front desk, out of earshot of the officer.

"Put him on speaker," Valentine said.

"Hello?" Louis's voice sounded hesitant.

I pressed the Facetime icon, and suddenly Louis appeared on the screen.

Before I could say anything, Franki asked, "What the heck is going on here, Armstrong?"

He blew out a breath. "It's not looking good at the moment. The police found something in Jim's belongings…"

"We know that. He told that to Kate hours ago. Do you know what they found?"

"A voodoo doll with a dolphin tail and a blowhole," Louis said.

"What?" I asked.

"Worse, apparently it's a doll that belonged to Delphine."

"A dolphin voodoo doll that belonged to Delphine," Franki repeated in a whisper.

Merry shrugged. "Caressa did say that Delphine believed in voodoo."

I looked from Merry to Louis. "What does the doll have to do with Jim? Why is that so incriminating?"

"For one thing," Louis shrugged in his oversized suit, "it proves he was with Delphine."

"Of course Jim was with Delphine!" My irritation was escalating. "That's why he was arrested."

"Wait, didn't Delphine say something about a curse?" Merry asked.

Valentine nodded. "In the security footage from the Burgundy Bar."

"Why would Delphine use a voodoo doll to curse herself?" I asked.

Franki shook her head. "She didn't. The dolphin voodoo doll belonged to Caressa, and she kept it in the pearl. That's what Delphine was referring to in the security footage when she accused Caressa of using hocus-pocus to kill her career."

She chewed her lip and then sighed. "Come on. Let's get out of here." She crossed the station toward the exit, the rest of us rushing to keep up. "We have to see Mambo Odette."

"Who?" Valentine asked.

Franki grimaced. "Odette Malveaux, a local voodoo priestess I'd rather not know."

"Wait!" I cried, getting everyone to stop. "What about Jim?"

Franki parked her hands on her hips, impatience etched on her face. "Sorry, Kate. Jim will have to wait."

MERRY

LESLIE LANGTRY

"Y ou know how to operate one of these?" Franki loomed over my shoulder as I studied the airboat controls.

Technically speaking, I knew how to *operate* an airboat. It's a good thing she didn't ask if I had experience *driving* one. I mean, I *had* driven one...once. This boat looked like that one, so I figured I could pull it off.

Alligator Snack Airboats was closest to the location of Mambo Odette's lair. Kate thought it was supposed to be the *Alligator Shack* because the top of the lowercase *h* appeared to have been gnawed off.

We were lucky since there were only two cars in the lot, and in one of them, someone sat reading a large newspaper. It looked like a slow day, and I was hoping the owner would take us to see Mambo Odette.

Remy Andre Arceneaux, the Cajun owner, disagreed, saying he wasn't taking people out on the swamp due to something he mumbled about the *cocodree* wanting *coulion andouille*. He was happy to rent us a boat and muttered something about us being *lagniappe* for the gators, but I might've misunderstood that.

"Oh sure." I exaggerated a smidge. "I totally know how to drive this. Carlos the Armadillo had an airboat. It's easy."

This was basically true. Carlos had bought the airboat for the annual Your Local Drug Cartel Appreciation Day Cookout and Sack Races event, which was odd because there wasn't a single body of water anywhere near his compound. There *was* a flooded rock quarry where they used to dump bodies, but it was really a deep water well surrounded by thirty-foot-high cliffs you couldn't scale. Besides, you wouldn't want to use it for water sports because of, you know, all the bodies.

Kate slowly lowered herself onto one of two benches in front of the driver's seat.

"Hold on." I jumped up and ran up the dock, shouting over my shoulder, "Be right back!"

The shack where we'd rented the boat was a new building poorly disguised to look like a rustic cabin. At the counter, I requested four headsets. I hesitated for a moment before pointing at a display.

"I'll need that one, too."

Remy nodded. "Now y'all don't feed dem gators." He turned away, but I could see his shoulders quaking with laughter.

Airboats were loud. Like, really loud. Carlos lost half of his hearing the first time he started his own airboat, and he never went near it again. Chloe the Clownfish, Sharkface Shawn, and I snuck it onto a trailer in the middle of the night and drove it ninety miles to a lake, where after five minutes of brilliant airboat driving, I crashed it into Pepe Ortega's—a rival cartel leader's—yacht.

Luckily, no one was on it, and the three of us managed to drive home before anyone noticed. The next morning, we told Carlos that Pepe had stolen his airboat. I kind of regretted starting that gang war.

Huh. I'd forgotten about crashing that vessel. I decided not to mention that to my friends.

Back in the boat, I handed out the headsets. "And this is for the babies." I carefully placed an oversized set of headphones on either side of Kate's belly. "I don't know where the twins' ears are, but safety first!"

"Where'd you find those?" Valentine smiled at the huge earphones that now straddled Kate's baby bump.

"On a giant stuffed alligator inside. You guys ready?" I jumped up into the driver's seat behind them. "Let's go!"

I turned the key in the ignition, and the fan roared to life. I eased forward on the steering stick, pressed the pedal with my foot, and we moved away from the dock. I wasn't too worried about where we were going because Franki was giving me directions.

Franki pointed out the broom-like cypress trees dripping with Spanish moss and various wildlife as we zoomed by. There were swamp rats called nutria, egrets, and other birds. The water was covered in places by some sort of floating vegetation, and I was careful to avoid rolling over logs.

"Stop!" Kate shrieked after about ten minutes, and I immediately stopped the boat.

"What's wrong?" Franki looked alarmed.

She had to be thinking what I was thinking...what if Kate went into labor in the middle of a swamp?

"Nothing," Kate said. "I just spotted some alligators!"

We followed her pointing finger to see four large gators in the distance, floating under a cypress tree.

Kate's bottom lip trembled. "Jim really wanted to see an alligator while he was down here."

"Do you want some photos with them?" Valentine stared with one part caution, one part courage from the gators to Kate who seemed to like this idea.

Kate smiled. "He'd love that."

She stood up and walked over to the front of the boat, leaning against the rail. The alligators stirred as Valentine took pictures of the pregnant woman with the large reptiles behind her.

"I don't think we're far from Odette's," Franki said.

"Merry?" Valentine warned, pointing at the water. "You should probably start this thing."

Four eight-foot-long alligators were writhing their way through the water toward us.

"They're used to tourists," Franki explained. "The tour boat operators probably feed them regularly so they'll come up to their boats."

"This is so cool!" Kate waddled to the end of the railing. "You never see stuff like this back home. We have sea lions on Pier 39, but they're not dangerous and don't try to eat tourists."

"We don't have any food," I mused. "I haven't seen any tour boats since we've been out here. Perhaps this isn't a normal route."

"They look hungry." Valentine reached into her bag and pulled out a straightening iron, gripping it defensively. She was ready to take on four alligators if they leaped up, each one much bigger than her. That was awesome.

Kate leaned over the edge of the boat as the vicious-looking alligators closed in. "Oh my gosh! How amazing is this?"

While it *was* amazing, I wondered if the gators were sizing up Kate and the twins as dinner and dessert. I turned the ignition key, but nothing happened. I tried two more times and got nothing.

"I don't suppose anyone has a gun?" I asked.

"Wouldn't do much good." Franki frowned. "Unless it's a hand cannon. Those hides are tough. Why do you think they make boots out of them?"

The alligators circled the boat menacingly. I'd rather have Kate's sea lions.

Kate bent lower toward the water. "Ooooh! You guys are adorable!"

One of the gators nudged the boat with his nose. The boat wobbled and so did Kate.

I didn't know how she did it so fast, but I watched in amazement as Valentine flung the barrel of the straightening iron around the safety bar like cowboys did with their reins outside a saloon.

The straightening iron looped around a couple of times until it hooked onto the bar. Holding onto the cord, Valentine grabbed Kate with her other hand and pulled her back upright.

"No cell service." Franki held up her phone before noticing the look on my face. "What is it?"

"I don't know if it's sabotage or a malfunction," I said slowly as it dawned on me. "It sure seems convenient though."

I scanned the swamp, hoping to see another boat. That was when I spotted it. In the far distance on the shore, was a person. With the setting sun shining behind the figure, I couldn't see very well to be certain, but it looked like the person was holding something to his or her face. Binoculars?

"Franki." I pointed to the shore.

"Oh good! Someone's spotted us." She waved her arms to get their attention. The shape on the shore didn't seem to pull out a phone. They merely watched us.

"I don't think they're going to help," I said. "I think someone hoped we'd get stuck out here." When could they have had the opportunity to sabotage us?

The person reading the paper in the car! Whoever it was saw us go into the *Alligator Snack*. They probably listened at the doorway and knew which boat we'd use. It wouldn't take much to sabotage the boat before we got onto it. But how'd they do it?

At the front of the boat, color was returning to Kate's cheeks. She'd really been through it today. Valentine wrapped up the iron and tucked it into her bag.

The alligators were still swarming around the boat. Franki swore under her breath and began to scour the boat for anything

163

we could use. I checked the fan blade—which looked okay—before turning my attention back to the control panel. Whatever it was had to be beneath it. There were four screws holding the cover in place.

"Are there any flathead screwdrivers on board?" I asked as I rummaged around.

"I have a nail file that's worked wonders in the past, especially if you use the tip for leverage." Valentine held the tool out to me and then looked at Franki, who was going through some sort of storage bin.

That might work. Easing the flat edge of the nail file into the slot, I began to loosen the first screw.

Valentine inched closer. "What's wrong?" she asked, quietly.

"Someone may have sabotaged the boat," I whispered as I pointed to the distant shore. "That guy, if I'm right."

Valentine shielded her eyes. "I can't tell if it's a man or woman. The sun's behind the person, so everything looks like a shadow."

The first screw popped off. The second one took more force. The third unscrewed easily, but the fourth was refusing to budge.

"Nothing useful here." Franki joined us. "I was hoping for a spear gun. There's not even water or a first-aid kit, which is weird because that stuff comes standard on these boats."

"No doubt, our saboteur cleaned out our options." I grunted and pushed hard, finally loosening the screw. "Okay!" The last screw came off, and I removed the panel. "Let's see what we can do to get this boat moving!"

Kate joined us and listened patiently as Franki filled her in. "I think our killer doesn't want us going to Mambo Odette's."

"And maybe not to come back at all." Franki nodded toward the four gators, who stayed with us. "Gators grab you and spin until you drown. Then they take you to the bottom of the swamp and bury you in the mud for later."

"Really?" Kate seemed fascinated.

Inside the panel I could see that a small, black box was attached to one of the wires. I tried to pry it off, but it was stuck tight.

"He LoJacked us." I leaned back. "Crap."

"What *is* it?" The others crowded around me.

I pointed at the box. "It's a GPS locator and kill switch. We used them back in the day to track people and stop their vehicle dead in its tracks. I'll keep it simple for the short time we have, but I think that guy," I motioned to the watcher on the shore, "attached the box to the wire. Once we got out here, he shut off the engine."

"Can we restart it?" Kate looked at the gators, who were boldly nudging the boat harder.

I sat back and contemplated our options. The boat rocked as all four alligators seemed to bump it at the same time. This was more dangerous than mud-wrestling an antique burlesque dancer, or taking on a few angry roller girls, especially because Caressa and the French Whorens weren't going to eat us once we were down.

I decided on a plan of action. "If we cut the wire before and after the kill-switch box and splice those ends together, the boat should start again. I've never done it before. I've never had to install one of these things...let alone remove it."

One of the gators put his chin on the edge of the boat. That didn't seem good. He didn't have permission to board.

"So, no oars or poles?" I asked.

Franki shook her head. "We don't have any of the standard equipment. Someone went to a lot of work to make sure we didn't have backup."

That wasn't great. "Valentine, do you have scissors?"

She frowned. "Of course." She reached into her bag and yanked something out. "How about cuticle clippers? They're sharp, and they snip well."

"That should work." I pulled the key from the ignition for

165

safety. "Cut the wire before and after the box, but not too short. We need enough to twist the two together."

I had Kate move to the central-most spot on the middle bench.

Two more alligators rested their chins on the edge of the boat as the last one tried to jump up onto it completely.

"Merry?" Franki asked, nervously. "What now?"

"This wire is really thick," Valentine said, hurrying. "But these cuticle clippers work on toenails. They should work on this. It'll take a minute though."

I watched Valentine put her muscle into it, then I answered Franki. "I'm not sure what's next. I was almost eaten by a couple of gators once in a bayou not far from here."

"I had a run-in with one once." Franki clenched her jaw. "How'd you get away?"

"I was rescued by a bigger alligator." I waved her off. "I'll tell you the rest another time. Right now, we need something to hit these guys with."

"What can I do?" Kate rose to her feet.

I held my hands up to stop her. "You're doing it. You have the most important job because you're keeping us balanced."

Kate smiled, patting her belly and sitting again. "I'm on it!"

"Found something!" Franki called out from under one of the benches. She got up and handed me a cheap lighter and a yard of heavy chain.

"How's it coming, Valentine?" I asked.

"Slowly." She bit her lip. "I'll keep at it!"

"You ready, Franki?"

"Nope." The PI scowled.

"All right." I gripped the thick, rusted chain. "I remember something from my last swamp tour. The guy said alligators don't like getting poked in the eyes or hit on the tip of their snout."

166

"That's it?" Franki asked. "I wish I had Nadezhda and her ax—make that just her ax."

"An ax would be nice," I admitted.

Kate was taking pictures as Valentine worked the cuticle clippers on the thick, rubber-coated wire.

The boat shook as one of the gators hauled himself up to his chest onto the boat. His mouth was closed. I only had a few seconds or he'd open it, clamp down on me, and drag me into the drink.

I raised my foot and stomped hard on the end of his muzzle. The gator slipped backward into the water with a look that asked *What did I ever do to you?*

"Merry!" Franki called out.

Another one had decided to jump on the boat. I whipped my chain and brought it down right between the eyes. Normally, I'd do whatever I could *not* to hurt an animal, but as far as I was concerned they'd brought this on themselves.

The gator slid back into the water just like the other one had.

I'd hoped my attacks on these two would discourage the others. I couldn't be more wrong. The two remaining alligators were on opposite sides and, simultaneously, as if they'd called each other the night before to organize the attack, lunged onto the boat.

"It's like that guy has them on a remote control or something," Franki complained.

I kept my eyes on the nearest reptile. "That happened to me once. But with llamas in Peru. This guy had two stuffed llamas on wheels, and there were three nuns…"

One of the gators pulled the rest of himself up onto the boat.

"I'll save that for later." I brought the chain down on the invader's head. It connected, but the reptile didn't retreat. Instead, he opened his mouth and hissed at me.

Valentine's bag was a few inches away. I snagged it and searched for what I hoped would be in there. Aha!

I held the lighter Franki had found up to the hairspray can I'd snatched from Valentine's bag, giving a silent prayer that the lighter wasn't empty. Aiming the can at the gator, I pressed both the nozzle and the lighter switch and launched a fireball right in front of the beast. The animal quickly jumped off the boat and, unlike the others, swam away.

I tossed the hairspray and lighter to Franki, who caught them. "I'm not getting close to that thing." She shook her head.

"Almost got it!" Valentine called out triumphantly, ignoring the sweat trickling down her forehead. She looked at Franki. "Isn't that my hairspray?"

The gator near Franki grumbled, and the PI tried to flick on the lighter, but it wouldn't work. She threw the can of hairspray and backed up. The can hit the gator in one eye, and he blinked.

It took me only a second to clamber over the bench and jump down in front of him. With a hard kick, I stomped on his muzzle. The reptile slid back into the water.

"Done!" Valentine shouted.

Franki joined her. "Do you have a small hair clip?"

Valentine's bag was proving very useful. Come to think of it, a hairstylist would make a great cover for a spy. They'd come with all their own weapons and could do your hair.

Valentine handed over a small, claw-like clip. Franki twisted the wires and, using the hair clip, clamped them together.

"Let's get out of here!" I called out as I raced back to my seat. I shoved the key into the ignition, and the engine roared, the propeller spinning until it was a blur.

Franki and Valentine sat on either side of Kate, and I steered us between two of the alligators and out further into the swamp.

"Look at that heron!" I shouted, pointing to a majestic bird on a stump. I was giddy with adrenaline, and the large white bird seemed like a beacon of hope and not being eaten.

"I've had enough of wildlife, thank you," Franki shouted back. "We need to head north!"

I sped up, and soon we were flying across the swamp. Franki gave me hand signals, and I followed them until we came to an enormous bald cypress. On the other side was an authentic, rundown shack with a porch and dock. On that porch was an old woman, standing, waiting for us. She had a brown turban on her head and was wearing a shapeless, muslin brown dress.

I slowed the boat.

"That's Mambo Odette," Franki told us. "Pull up to the dock."

The voodoo priestess was so still I thought she was a statue. As I steered the boat alongside the dock, she moved. She took the rope from me and tied it around a post so brittle it looked like one slight breeze would turn it into dust.

"Been waitin'," the woman said in a husky alto. "You'd best come in. I know whatcha want."

Franki and Valentine stepped up onto the dock. I stayed on the boat and among the three of us, we managed to get Kate out of the boat safely.

Mambo Odette cocked her head to one side when she saw the pregnant woman. Without a word, she placed both hands on Kate's belly and closed her eyes.

"Twins are goin ta be jes fine," she murmured before opening her eyes. "They say they's happy in there, but want you not ta rock the boat next time."

How could she know that? I climbed onto the dock and wasn't quite sure what to do. How does one politely introduce oneself to a voodoo queen? I'd met unusual folks before, from the keeper of Putin's favorite riding bear to a naked Uruguayan monk from the Church of the Unenlightened Ocelot. But this was a new experience for me.

Mambo Odette turned her attention to Valentine. She reached out and took a few strands of my friend's glossy, long locks in her hand. Valentine smiled and started to introduce herself, but Mambo held up her hand to silence her.

The priestess closed her eyes and mumbled in a language I wasn't familiar with. Then she opened her eyes.

"May I ask what you said?" Valentine asked in a way so polite there was no way Odette could be offended.

"Ah was wondrin' what ya could do with my hair. It's been long time since ah had a trim." Odette turned and frowned at Franki. "*You* again. I know whatcha want. Ya better go in."

The other three went into the shack, but the voodoo priestess stopped me from following them. She took my hand in hers and closed her eyes. If she had the *sight,* she'd probably say something sage about how all the roads I'd traveled around the world just led me back home.

She opened her eyes, and I awaited the wisdom.

"The gators think ya're mean," was all she said before she turned and went into the shack.

Okay. That was fair.

My phone buzzed. Looking through the doorway, I could see my friends checking out the inside of the shack. Mambo Odette was explaining to Kate that the zodiac sign of the twins was very important to making sure they wouldn't grow up to be psycho killers. She was recommending a daily dose of powdered rat eyeball, which she happened to have...for a price.

Kate looked at her phone and stepped out of the shack. Was cell service back? I decided to hazard a look at my phone. It was another text stream from the girls.

How important is it that you have Rufus? Betty asked.

I love Rufus! I replied. Well...as much as anyone could love an impotent poison dart frog.

But on a scale of 1 to 1,599...with 1 being the highest score, the girl added.

I gritted my teeth. *Dr. Wulf told me you 'liberated' my frog into the zoo exhibit.*

There was a pause.

She shouldn't have done that, came the reply. *Now we have to kill her.*

Nope, I texted back. *No one is killing anyone.*

I'm just kidding, Betty replied. *But seriously. You have to give a rating.*

I responded instantly. *One! One is the rating.*

So you don't want your frog, Betty concluded. *I guess it's good we found him a new home.*

What do you mean? Lauren texted. *We haven't found him yet!*

Don't tell her that! Betty warned.

Inez chimed in. *Maybe he's hitchhiking back to Costa Rica?*

First off, I texted, *the number one is supposed to be the highest score.*

Betty texted. *No it isn't.*

You said that! I text-shouted.

She denied it. *No I didn't.*

You kind of did, Ava typed.

You shouldn't confuse Mrs. Wrath, one of the Kaitlyns added. *She's super old.*

I'm not that old, and I understand you just fine, I texted in my defense. *You guys lost my frog, so you guys have to find him.*

He's in the exhibit somewhere, Lauren explained. *We just hope he didn't end up in the alligator area. They might attack him. Alligators are dangerous, you know.*

They had no idea.

Find my frog, please, I texted before pocketing my phone.

And then I went through the doorway and joined the others inside the shack.

RING CAMERA VIDEO

DIANA ORGAIN

*E*XTERIOR – Mid-Morning, backyard.

A man, only visible from the waist down, dressed in tan pants, slowly exits the building from the back door and advances toward a woman standing poolside. She is wearing a bustle skirt with a large dolphin tail attached and blue kitten heels. The woman has various veins and swollen ankles, giving away that she is well past middle-age.

The man stops in front of the woman. The woman's hands wave dramatically toward the man in an accusatory fashion. His hands gesture angrily back. After another moment of intense arm waving, the man slaps his hands to his legs and slowly walks away.

LATER

The woman slips out of view, then reappears and enters the house through the back door.

MINUTES PASS

The same woman with the swollen ankles, wearing the dolphin tail, comes out the back door, holding a large pearl. She goes toward the gate, then stops as a man with tan pants enters and backs her toward the pool.

. . .

THE MAN STOPS and hands the woman a phone. They stay in this position for several minutes as if having a conversation. Finally, the man yanks the pearl out of the woman's hands. His arms rise, and the pearl disappears from view. A second later, the woman's knees buckle, and she crumbles to the ground. Her phone drops beside her.

The pearl falls to the ground and cracks open. An object flies from the pearl and lands in the grass. The man picks up the phone, turns slightly toward the camera, wipes off the phone, and shoves it into his shirt pocket. Unceremoniously, he kicks the dolphin woman and the pearl halves into the pool.

He scurries out the gate.

LATER

A man in tan pants slowly enters the frame. He pauses. Back to the camera, he bends and picks up an object from the grass. He pockets it, then heads for the back door. He stops suddenly, swivels toward the pool, and strides toward it. He yanks out a cell phone from his pocket and dials.

FRANKI

TRACI ANDRIGHETTI

"Y ou wan' ta know about da doll." Mambo Odette's undead tone matched her lifeless eyes.

"Personally"—Merry gestured to a voodoo altar with a skull in the top hat of the notorious *loa* of the underworld, Baron Samedi—"I'd love to know about Abe Lincoln here, too."

Mambo Odette struck a long match on her calloused palm and shuffled to an oil lamp that hung above a makeshift table in the center of the one-room shack. She lit the wick, and the other residents of the altar leaped into view like items from a horror movie. An antique doll torso with a glassy gaze, a severed alligator head and chicken feet, a mummified creature in a cape.

My eyes locked onto a primitive voodoo doll with pins. It didn't have a dolphin tail or blowhole, but they would've been easy to add.

The voodoo priestess continued around the space, lighting candles placed on wood scraps nailed to the walls.

The sun had set so I appreciated the light, even though it *had* revealed the altar contents. I glanced out the only window in the shack and saw Kate staring intently at her phone.

I took a seat at the table and waited for Mambo Odette to join me. Nothing had changed since the last time I'd visited her home. Besides the altar and the table, there was a cot, a washstand, and a cabinet full of jars containing substances best left unidentified.

Valentine picked up a jar labeled *Sample – Not for Sale*. "What's this?"

Mambo Odette didn't respond, so I stepped in. "That's her swamp mud skin cream. A local witch named Theodora says it works magic on the complexion." I smirked before uttering the next sentence. "She claims to be three hundred years old but doesn't look a day over fifty-nine."

"Ooh." Valentine unscrewed the cap. "I wonder if it can be used as a hair mask."

Judging from its burned perm hair smell, I wouldn't risk it.

Mambo Odette lit a plate of herbs on the table, and a black, acrid smoke invaded the air like a demonic spirit. She extinguished the match with her fingers and eased into the seat across from me.

She was a woman of few words, not to mention one who spoke in veiled messages, so I decided to get to the point. "Why did you give Caressa a dolphin effigy that she could use against Delphine?"

"I don' make da decisions. Da *loa* do."

That was debatable, but far be it from me to argue with a voodoo practitioner.

"Did Caressa say why she wanted the doll?"

Her black eyes went reptilian. "You know da answer ta dat, chile."

Right. To kill Delphine's career. But my gut told me I was missing something, as did Mama Esther's frightened reaction to the bone throw. "Mama Esther in the Quarter said that Erzulie d'en Tort is angry. Since Erzulie seeks revenge on behalf of women who've been wronged, why didn't she get even with Caressa for wronging Delphine?"

"She did."

175

"How?"

Her lips stretched into what might've been a smile. "Caressa been writin' in mud for decades, and she don' die."

Merry tilted her head. "When you look at it that way, it *does* seem like payback."

Excellent point. But I wondered whether my nonna had been right that Delphine was out for vendetta. "What about Delphine? Did she ever come to you for help with Caressa?"

"She come 'round for a love potion. Took her man." Mambo Odette rose and went outside.

Valentine looked at me. "Odette was talking about Eduardo." She returned the swamp mud to the cabinet. "We should go after her."

"Do we have to?" The skull asked in the voice of Merry, who worked its jaw. "This voodoo altar is the bomb."

Yeah, as in a jolt to the senses. "Mambo Odette knows something she's not saying."

I rose from the table. "We need to join Kate outside. The name *Alligator Snack Airboats* is no accident. For those gators we ran into earlier, Kate's a three-piece combo from Willie's Chicken Shack."

Merry put Baron Samedi on the altar, and we went outside. The voodoo priestess was near the water, stoking coals beneath a stock pot.

"Guys!" Kate emerged from the side of the building, waving her phone. "Louis Armstrong sent me a Ring video from Glenda's mansion, and it shows the murder."

Valentine blinked wide-eyed, long eyelashes fluttering.

Merry eyed the phone. "Well? Who offed the dolphin?"

"I'm not sure." Kate held up the display. "The camera only shows everyone from the waist down."

Leave it to Caressa to aim the camera at the genital area. "Glenda told me that Caressa had gotten rid of the security camera."

"Thank goodness she was wrong," Kate said, "because the video proves Jim's innocent. Look." She pressed Play, and we watched the video where a scuffle ensued—or at least, the bottom half of one—between someone in a dolphin tail and kitten heels and a man in baggy tan pants.

Kate paused the video. "See the wide legs? Jim doesn't own pants like that."

Relief filled my chest. "Glenda doesn't own *any* pants."

"Wait a minute." Valentine crossed her arms and tapped her polished nails on her toned biceps, her eyes narrowed on the screen. "If that was Jim in the first frame, waving his arms at Delphine, his pants don't look that much more tailored than the assailant's. The only clear difference is that Jim's walk was slower, and judging by the length of his legs, I'd say he's another four or five inches taller than the murderer."

She licked her frosted lip, as if thinking about this some more. "Unfortunately, someone who walked fast or slow in a video might not be enough to make a conviction. As for height, all the other suspects seem to have the same stature."

"Hang on." Merry squinted at the screen. "I've seen those pants before."

I blinked. "On whom? Boris Johnson?"

"No, Kim Jong-un wore them as a bathing suit on his waterslide yacht to celebrate the vaFoundation of the Korean Workers' Party holiday. He didn't really care about the workers, but he did love an excuse for a party."

We could hardly pin the murder on the North Korean dictator, and Valentine had made some valid points about the height difference in the men and the pace they were walking. It seemed as if the slightly larger men's trousers were what we had to go on, and the fact that Delphine's killer had to be an old man.

Buddy?

Tibs?

Eduardo?

Arthur?

Even though I'd ruled out Glenda's involvement, I had questions about Caressa. She could've used her crawdad queen wiles to get any one of the men to do her bidding.

"There's more." Kate resumed the video, and an object flew to the grass.

Valentine studied the screen. "What was that?"

"I had to watch it a few times to figure it out," Kate said, "but it's the voodoo doll flying from the pearl, likely after it hit Delphine over the head."

The unmistakable—and untimely—odor of death made us all turn to the water. It was coming from the stock pot.

Merry's lips thinned. "I'd better go find out what—or who—died." She walked to the boiling concoction and peered in. "What's cookin', Odette?"

"Gumbo." She raised a spoonful. "River rat an' black swamp snake."

Merry patted her belly. "I really couldn't. Kate?"

Kate turned the greenish color of the water and shook her head. It was the first time any of us had seen her refuse food.

Mambo Odette tasted the swamp stew. "Gumbo work its voodoo, like dem dolls."

Gumbo *was* magical—just not the river rat and black swamp snake version. But I didn't believe anyone could harm another by sticking pins into a doll. "No offense, but either the victim of a doll brings the voodoo on themselves, or the possessor of the doll takes other steps to make sure bad things happen to their victim. In this case, both apply. Delphine's drinking hurt her career, but Caressa also prevented her from dancing."

"Speaking of bad things happening," Kate raised her phone, "now that we know about this video, we need to go to Central Lockup and demand they release Jim."

Given how dangerous the trip to the shack had been, I

dreaded the return voyage. The four of us had barely escaped those gators.

Wait.

My eyes darted to the airboat, then I turned to Mambo Odette. "How did Caressa get out here? Surely she didn't come alone."

She sniffed and gazed at the swamp. "Sometime ta git where ya want ta go, ya need someone dat know da ropes."

Not a specific answer, but it told me what I'd suspected. Someone had brought Caressa to see Mambo Odette. Still, the *know the ropes* phrase gave me pause because it sounded like one of the voodoo priestess's coded messages.

"Kate's right, Franki." Valentine pointed at the boat, revealing a dab of what appeared to be Mambo Odette's swamp mud on her wrist. "We should be on our way."

My skin tingled as though pricked by pins, and the coded message cracked open like Caressa's pearl.

The wrist.

I pulled out my phone. Thankfully, there was a weak signal. I dialed Glenda.

"What's shakin', sugar?" she answered.

Honestly, *I* was shaking, but I didn't say that. "I need a favor. Where are you?"

"Buddy and Tibs are driving me to the fourplex now. My departure from the Burgundy Bar was delayed. After I won the straddle-off, I stayed to treat the patrons to a free show."

I thought she already had. "Perfect. Have them pick up your mother, Arthur, Concepción, and Eduardo and drive them to the mansion. And don't let anyone leave before I get there."

"I take it you have news about Miss Delphine?"

My gaze shifted to the swamp water, and I flashed back to the filthy swimming pool. "Close. Her murderer."

"SEEING THE SUSPECTS TOGETHER IS SURREAL." Kate peered into Glenda's living room through the gold curtains in the entryway. "It's like a theater-style Agatha Christie reveal."

Valentine rose from the bottom stair and picked up her beauty bag, ready for catch-a-killer duty. "Except that instead of an elegant 1930's mansion, the place looks like a French brothel."

"French?" Merry slid down the stripper pole. "With all that animal print, it's more African Safari bordello."

Whatever the decór, I was happy to be out of that Caramel Cat dress, otherwise I would've blended with the furnishings. "As we discussed on the boat, I'll nod when it's time to execute the plan. Are we ready?"

Kate chewed her nail. "I don't know, Franki. Should we wait for Detective Mangiaratti and Louis Armstrong?"

"Definitely not. People are less inclined to talk in front of police, and Louis is likely to spout off some legalese and blow everything."

Merry parted the curtain. "Ladies, it's showtime."

We filed into the hot-pink room and faced the seating area. Glenda, Caressa, and Buddy sat on the tiger rococo couch, while Tibs paced. Concepción and Eduardo were in the cheetah and leopard armchairs. Arthur leaned against the wall by the lewd leg lamp, chewing a toothpick.

The hostile stares of the suspects were a stark reminder that this was no mystery theater. One wrong move, and someone else could share Delphine's fate. "Thank you all for coming."

"As if we had a choice," Concepción hissed. She shot daggers at Buddy and Tibs. "Those dirty old men manhandled me."

Glenda, who wore an outfit made entirely of black elastic bands with the word BADDIE across her chest, crossed her legs and kicked a BEYOTCH boot. "I'm disappointed in you boys." Her wrinkled lips assumed a playful pout. "I didn't get so much as a pinch on my posterior."

Eduardo snorted. "Would one of you tell us what this is

about? It's ten o'clock at night, and I have an important meeting tomorrow."

"I'll give you a hint," Caressa drawled. "We're not here to play Strippopoly."

"What's that?" Kate rubbed the small of her back. "A strip version of Monopoly?"

Glenda braced her BADDIE BEYOTCH self against the tiger-striped cushions. "There's a non-strip version?"

"You know," Kate said, "do not pass go, do not collect two hundred dollars?"

"Evidently, you weren't playing Strippopoly when you got knocked up." Glenda adjusted a strap. "Everyone knows you collect three C-notes when you draw a BUSTED!! card from the His or Hers pile."

"His and Hers?" Valentine frowned. "They're called the 'Chance' and 'Community Chest' cards."

"Heh!" Buddy slapped his thigh. "A chance at the community chest."

Tibs leered. "I like the sound of that."

Kate silenced the men with a side-eye. "Whatever the cards are called, the result is the same. You go to jail."

"Jail?" Glenda shouted. "Lawd, child. No one goes to *jail* in Strippopoly. They go to the strip club, and they can't put on any clothing."

To pre-empt a possible demonstration, I raised my hands. This wasn't what Kate had meant by an Agatha Christie *reveal*. "We didn't bring you all here to discuss games," I said, although I kind of wondered if the Strippoply money was all ones. "We're here to solve Delphine's murder."

Arthur removed the toothpick. "We're not here to *play* games, either. The police have the killer."

"It wasn't my Jim." Kate perched on an arm of the couch. "We have proof."

Concepción looked from Kate to Caressa, and her brown eyes

turned black. "*You*. You destroyed her career, and you were fighting at the bar on the day she died. Then she was murdered here at your old mansion."

"I didn't need to kill her career. Delphine's dolphin act was dead in the water."

Literally, I thought, remembering her body in the pool out back.

Arthur nodded. "She was a fish out of water in the burlesque business."

Actually, a mammal. But, again, I kept that fact to myself. I walked over to Caressa. "You weren't lying when you said you didn't do anything to Delphine. You did it to the dolphin voodoo doll you got from Mambo Odette and which you kept in the pearl."

"The one you killed her with," Concepción said.

All eyes were on Caressa, who was as calm as a clam. "Like I told Franki in my dressing room, Delphine brought her troubles on herself when she started drinking, and when she hooked up with him."

Caressa's arm began to rise.

Everyone leaned forward, waiting to see who she would point to. Finally, her finger indicated Eduardo.

"You're still jealous," he said with a growl.

Caressa turned as red as a crawdad, and a couple of her wig curls bounced like antennae. "At first. But you and I both know Delphine did me a favor."

Merry's lips thinned. "Because the visiting Spanish dignitary, a.k.a. the former king's cousin, isn't as dignified as he wants people to think. He's a failed Hollywood talent agent named George."

Eduardo-slash-George tugged at his opera scarf and looked away.

I got in his face. "When you lent your fake Spanish identity to Mexican booze, the city got wind of your visit and invited you to the Running of the Bulls. Neither you nor Concepción was happy about that because she was a Roller Girl, and you both worried someone would out you before you could collect on the tequila deal. And, ironically, that person was Concepción when she called you George in earshot of the event announcer."

Kate rose and approached Concepción. "You didn't stay away from the event because you knew I'd made a video of the security footage from the Burgundy Bar. You had your French Whoren teammates help you steal my phone."

She crossed her arms but didn't meet Kate's gaze. "I was trying to find out what had happened to my *abuelita*."

"You sure?" I asked. "Or were you trying to find out what was in the pearl?"

Kate pointed at Concepción. "Don't try to deny it. I heard you on the phone saying, 'It's gone!' and 'Now what do we do?' You knew your grandmother went to the mansion to get something Caressa had, and you thought it was something of value, like jewelry or cash."

"Not only that," Valentine said, "you sounded like a gold digger in a recording of your last phone conversation with Delphine."

Concepción turned pale. "A recording?"

I pulled the plastic baggie with Delphine's phone from my back pocket. "The killer stole your grandmother's cell from the Burgundy Bar, and it has a recording of the two of you talking. I found this in the back of Buddy and Tibs's limo."

"That proves I didn't kill her." Concepción moved to the edge of her chair. "Tonight was the first time they've given me a ride."

"Me, too," Eduardo said.

Arthur returned the toothpick to the corner of his mouth. "I've never been in one of their limos until today, either."

"My mother and I have many times." Glenda pulled a cigarette holder from a BEYOTCH boot. "But we didn't kill Delphine."

"No, you didn't." I surveyed the other suspects. "We have Ring camera video from the backyard that proves the killer is a male, one of the men in this room."

The men stiffened and sized up one another.

Glenda glared at Caressa. "Mother! You told me you canceled the Ring service."

"You shouldn't have believed that nonsense. I had to keep an eye on you because I didn't want the neighbors to think I'd sold my house to a whore."

My lips pursed. Glenda had said something similar to me when I'd rented her apartment.

Concepción stood and stormed to me. "I demand to know who is on the video."

Louis Armstrong came through the curtains. "It only shows people from the waist down, so she couldn't tell you."

Groans erupted from the girls, and I squeezed my hands to keep from wrapping them around the lippy lawyer's neck. "Never represent a client at trial, Louis. You'll disappoint your mother."

Eduardo rose and joined his granddaughter. "Delphine pressed charges against the limo drivers for following her. They're the killers."

Merry raised a hand. "Slow down, Eddie. Or Georgie. Buddy and Tibs are stalkers, not killers."

"I can accept that," Buddy said.

"Yeah." Tibs jutted out his lower lip. "I'm good."

Arthur headed for the curtains. "I don't have time for this. I'm out."

Merry and I blocked his exit, and I pointed to his wrist. "I've met enough sailors at local pirate festivals to know that deck-hands often get a coiled rope tattoo."

He rubbed his wrist. "So I was a Marine. What does that prove?"

"Nothing. But Mambo Odette said someone who 'knew the ropes' took Caressa to her house on the swamp to get the voodoo doll. If Caressa doesn't identify you, Mambo Odette will."

"It was him," Caressa said flatly.

Arthur pointed his toothpick at me. "Hold on. I didn't go inside her shack, and I never saw any doll."

"Maybe not, but the way you slunk behind the bar to steal Delphine's phone proves you're not just a thief, you're a sneak who spied on Caressa as well as Delphine."

Kate aimed her cell at him. "And you wore a black glove, not because you were worried about fingerprints, but because the security camera would've captured your tattoo."

Arthur glanced at the curtains, as though plotting an escape. "What reason would I have had to kill Delphine?"

"You loved her." Valentine's eyes narrowed. "But she jilted you."

Merry crossed her arms. "My guess is you didn't want Delphine to dance anymore because she met so many men. So you sabotaged her behind the scenes and blamed it on Caressa."

He stepped forward, but I blocked him from going any further. "And this morning Delphine had had enough. She broke into the mansion and figured out the voodoo doll was inside the pearl. You followed her here and realized the jig was up. Caressa no longer had anything on her, and neither did you. At that point, you did what you should've done decades ago—you declared your love. She spurned you, and you lost your temper and hit her over the head with the pearl."

"That's right," Kate said. "The doll flew out, and Jim found it when he came back from his walk."

Arthur laughed, his pupils enlarged. "A black-gloved phone theft, a video filmed from the waist down. You sleuths sure ain't Miss Marples, or Jessica Fletchers, for that matter. And remember, I've never been in one of the old geezers' limos."

"No," I said, "but after you stole Delphine's phone from the bar, you went to give it back to her at the mansion. After you killed her, you recaptured the phone and put it in your shirt pocket, probably for safekeeping, and when you later carried

Caressa from the dressing room to the limo, bending to slide her into the car, it fell onto the floor."

Arthur shoved past me, and I nodded at the girls to execute our plan.

Merry removed Caressa's glasses to keep her from seeing what we were about to do.

Kate clamped her hand over Louis's mouth.

Valentine pulled a baggie with Ariel from her beauty bag. "This is the voodoo doll that was inside the pearl, and it has your fingerprints on it."

Arthur turned. "That's not the doll. It's not even a...."

"Dolphin?" I suggested. "You're right. It's Ariel from *The Little Mermaid*, and you've just incriminated yourself."

He pushed Louis and then Kate, eliciting gasps from the guests. Then he fled into the entryway.

Chaos and shouts ensued as we all gave pursuit—except for Caressa, who needed extra time. The four of us made it to the entryway first. Merry and Valentine ran around Arthur to block the door. Kate and I blocked the hallway to the back door. Louis, Concepción, and Glenda dashed through the curtains, followed by Buddy, Tibs, and Eduardo.

Surrounded, Arthur pulled a gun and backed into the stairs to cover us all. "Clear the doorway," he said to Merry and Valentine, "and everyone survives the night."

Anxiety compressed my gut like Caressa's foot had my cheek. I had to do something to protect my friends. "Don't do anything stupid, Arthur. The police are on their way."

"She's right, sailor." Merry shrugged. "Won't do you any good to run now."

Valentine shot him a scowl. "You won't get away with killing Delphine."

Kate clenched her fists. "Or with ruining Jim's and my vacation, which had already gotten off to a bad start." She glared at Glenda. "By the way, we still want a refund."

"Over my dead body, Katie, honey. It's practically tomorrow."

Concepción gasped. "You have some nerve using that expression."

"What?" Glenda was taken aback. "Your grandma might be dead, but I've got to make a living."

Concepción went RollerBull on Glenda, who assumed a BADDIE BEYOTCH stripper straddle-off squat.

"Knock it off, you two," Arthur shouted.

Taking advantage of the distraction, I gripped the stripper pole. With a heave, I swung and kicked the gun from his hand.

Glenda straddled Concepción and put a hand to her heart, smiling at me. "Tiger Eye's not a tiger. She's an ol' polecat, just like me."

I'd have to straighten out the animal issue later, because this wasn't the time. Merry and Arthur were on the ground, wrestling for the gun.

Kate plunked down onto Arthur's back, her face a ball of rage.

"Help!" He waved an arm and kicked his feet. "I'm being crushed by a whale."

Merry grabbed the gun and pressed the barrel to his temple. "Insult a pregnant woman again, and it's the last thing you say."

Caressa finally emerged through the curtains, and we all patiently waited while she recreated the wrestling move she'd used on me—a foot into Arthur's cheek. "Serves you right for falling in love with a dolphin, Flipperophile freak."

I helped Kate up and turned to Buddy, Tibs, and Eduardo. "Take Arthur to the dining room and tie him up in one of the bondage chairs."

The front door burst open, and we all spun, expecting Mangiaratti and his men with guns drawn.

Instead, it was David and The Vassal in their brown faux fur bowcaster holders. They raised what looked like a cross between a bow and a sling shot and pelted Arthur with painted bandolier blocks.

I didn't ask why they were wearing their Krewe of Chewbacchus Mardi Gras costumes in July, because in New Orleans it wasn't weird. "That's enough, guys. We've already subdued the culprit."

They lowered their Wookiee weaponry, and Buddy, Tibs, and Eduardo dragged a dazed Arthur down the hall.

"How'd you two know where I was?" I asked.

David brushed his bangs from his eyes. "Veronica sent us to see if you were here. She got worried when Bradley called and said he couldn't get a hold of you to let you know his flight is coming in late tonight."

I pulled my phone from my pocket. "I forgot to charge the battery when we got back from the swamp."

A police car pulled up.

Louis pointed at me. "Now you're in trouble. I can list a series of offenses you've committed."

"Incitement?" I asked.

He thought for a moment. "No, that's not one of them."

"Now it is." I turned to David and The Vassal. "Take our attorney friend out back and give him a personal demonstration of how your bowcasters work."

"Hey!" He pointed at me. "That's also a threat!"

"Yes." Merry stared him down. "I believe so."

Louis ran for the back door, and the boys went after him.

Mangiaratti strutted up the walkway like he owned the property. "What's this about you gathering the suspects, Amato? You know I could charge you for interfering in an investigation."

"You could, but then you wouldn't be able to take the credit for solving it." I patted him on the shoulder. "FYI, the stagehand did it."

Merry handed him the gun. "This is his. We've got to run."

"Yes." Valentine slipped Ariel into her beauty bag. "We're on our way to get Jim out of Central Lockup, so don't anyone stop us."

"I'm so excited." Kate gave a squeal. "I read there's a charming Creole eatery on the way."

Merry looked at me. "It *is* past dinnertime, and we never had that fancy lunch."

I decided to roll with the dinner detour. After all, *laissez les bons temps rouler* was a New Orleans motto. "I know the place. They make a good Andouille sausage gumbo."

Kate turned the color of Mambo Odette's river rat and black swamp snake version. "On second thought, we should follow the rules of non-strip Monopoly."

Laughing, we headed for my Mustang. "Go to jail," we recited. "Go directly to jail."

EPILOGUE: VALENTINE

ARLENE MCFARLANE

"Thanks for the framed picture of Pirate's Alley," Max gushed, pressing the gift to his chest. He pulled it back and studied it for the umpteenth time. "I *love* it!"

"It's the least I could do, considering you held things together here while I was in New Orleans."

He straightened and set the picture on his station beside a jar of Barbicide. "I did, didn't I?"

As much as I'd enjoyed the trip to New Orleans, it was good to be home. Where else could I rely on humor and sarcasm in such rapid succession? After landing at Boston's Logan Airport in good time, I figured I'd see if help was needed at the salon since it'd be open.

Max was still gazing gaga-like over the picture. "Did you know modern-day pirates visit that area to swashbuckle at various local festivals?"

Thanks to Franki's generous explanation, I did know that, but no need to burst Max's bubble. "You don't say!"

"It's true. Maybe one day I'll take in one of those events." He puffed out his chest, chin high. "I'd have made a good pirate." He

190

did the *en garde* stance. "Take *that!*" He pounced, jabbing me with a pretend sword.

I giggled at his display. As animated as Max was, he was more Mr. Smee than Captain Hook, sort of a sweet, harmless pirate— with a keen fashion sense.

I peered at the clock. "Where are Jock and Phyllis? It's only five-thirty."

"Phyllis said she'd had enough for the day. And since she gave Mrs. Hartounian a major case of breakage after her perm as well as losing a bunch of feathers from her French maid's duster in the poor woman's hair, I'd suggested we'd *all* had enough."

I rolled my eyes. Here I'd thought *I* had shedding-feather problems. Phyllis's issues could top mine in a heartbeat.

"And Jock?" I gave a casual glance around the salon.

"He followed her home. Her car was sputtering again. Myself, I would've let her go alone, but you know Jock. Navy hero. Superman. God's gift to...well, everyone."

I kept a neutral look on my face though inside I shivered at all the things Jock was—in abundance.

"Anyway, lovey!" Max clasped his hands in glee. "Huge congratulations are in order!"

I plopped my bag by my station and unloaded my tools. "For what?"

"The judges from the L'Amour Hair Show contest called and left a message that you and your Ariel mermaid creation won the category for Best Imagination!"

"What? *Get! Out!*" I slapped both palms on his chest, shocked to say the least. Although, I had to admit, it was true. I did have a pretty good imagination. Wasn't always a plus in the life of Valentine Beaumont, but there it was. "This doesn't make sense. You should've seen the Marie Antoinette hairdo. That model had two feet of white curls on top of her head. Not to mention bows and flowers intricately placed on each level, like a wedding cake."

"Well, your fins and sparkles clearly outdid them all. They

said they were looking for a fresh touch, not something that was copying an old look."

Huh. Go figure. Wait till I shared this news with Merry and the other sleuths.

"How are we going to celebrate?" Max wanted to know.

"I think we'll celebrate in private," came a sexy male voice from behind that I knew all too well.

I quivered from the deep, suggestive tone and whipped around, spying Romero, arms crossed, leaning against the sales counter by the front door. He had a leather jacket on his back, gun at his hip, and dark waves spilling over his collar. He strode a foot toward me, his penetrating gaze fixed on my face.

English twin sisters—regulars in the salon—sitting side by side under the dryers, looked up from their magazines at the virile, irresistible cop in my life. Their eyes got big and round at his hard-assed swagger and the seductive look on his face. They inhaled sharply and simultaneously sighed in delight, leaving dreamy smiles on their faces.

I knew the feeling. A hot rush surged through my body at the sight of this man. "I beg your pardon?" I teased.

"You heard me. I should've cuffed you to my bedpost when I had the opportunity. Maybe *that* would've kept you from getting into any more trouble."

The women squeaked in surprise at his words. Wait, that was me.

I grabbed my bag from my station, giving myself a moment to compose myself, then moseyed over to him, and wrapped my arms around his toned waist.

I blinked up at him coyly, giving an extra flutter through my long lashes. "You didn't expect me to let a murderer get away scot-free, did you?"

He kissed the tip of my nose, playing along. "Not on your life."

"Well, if it's a celebration you want, I have something to show you."

192

He looked from me to my bag. "Does it have to do with a striptease and pink feathers?"

I turned and looked down at one of the feathers from my memorable act that had clearly migrated into my bag and was now poking out. "Uh, actually it does. But we may have to get creative with the feathers."

EPILOGUE: KATE

DIANA ORGAIN

I kissed Jim for the umpteenth time. My affection was so over-the-top that my friend and rival PI Vicente Domingo (who'd taken the red-eye from San Francisco to help with the case—only to find that the killer foursome didn't need his help) said, "Knock it off. I already feel like a third wheel."

"I'm sorry it didn't work with Concepción," I said to Vicente.

He laughed and shrugged it off, eyeing a shapely redhead walking in front of us. "No worries, Kate. It always works out for me."

"Anne Rice let you all in on some secrets of this city," our vampire tour guide said. "Across the street is the home of Lestat, well, in the Hollywood movie anyway."

I shuddered, and Jim wrapped a protective arm around my waist. "Are you cold, Kate?"

"No," I said. "I'm fascinated. Did I ever tell you how I read all those vampire novels in high school and walked around with garlic in my backpack?"

Jim snorted. "You? Scared? I don't believe it."

I laughed. "As a teen, I was deathly afraid of vampires. Yet I couldn't stop myself from reading those novels."

194

The tour guide continued. "This is the home where the family *over* for dinner *became* dinner."

"I'm not interested in dinner," Vicente said.

Jim chuckled and then whispered in my ear. "I think Vicente is distracted."

"I'm more interested in a drink." Vicente was loud enough for a particular redhead to hear.

The woman glanced over her shoulder and made eye contact with Vicente, whom, I must say, with his dark hair and black leather jacket, looked quite mysterious himself.

"I don't think he's three-wheeling anymore," Jim said.

I snuggled into my husband. "Truth is, he was never a third wheel." I rubbed my belly. "More like a fifth wheel."

The tour guide moved our group down the street. "Now on to St. Marty's Chapel. I'll tell you the story of two tourists who thought they'd sit outside the chapel all night in folding chairs to see which of its shutters opened and why. They thought they'd be rich finding the answer, but they were found in the morning lifeless and bloodless."

The redhead hesitated in following, and Vicente sidled up to her to make small talk.

"I'm sorry our trip went screwy, honey," Jim said.

I laced my fingers through his as we followed our guide down a dark alley. "It's not your fault."

He gave my hand a reassuring squeeze. "I'm glad I'm married to the smartest PI in town."

At the mention of a PI, Vicente glanced over at us. "*Que?*"

"I did have help from some very savvy ladies," I said.

Before Jim could reply, the tour guide said something about a haunting and ghosts, then a strong wind whipped through the alley, making my hair stand on end.

The redhead shrieked and, to Vicente's delight, grabbed his arm.

I snuggled closer to Jim.

He quirked an eyebrow at me. "Have you had enough of this ghost tour?"

"It *is* getting late," I said, "and we still need to have that romantic dinner I promised you."

Because Vicente had ears in the back of his head, he turned toward us. "Of course! Kate needs to get off her feet. We need to feed her." He wrapped his arm around the redhead. "I know a great Spanish restaurant in town. *Vamonos!*"

I glanced at Jim's smiling face. Warmth filled me just looking at him. "What do you think?"

Jim chuckled. "I say the food Maserati gave me in jail was the worst I've ever had. *Vamonos!*"

EPILOGUE: MERRY

LESLIE LANGTRY

"And after they dyed my cat orange, they lost my golden poison dart frog at the zoo..." I explained to the elderly nun sitting next to me on my flight out of New Orleans, bound for Iowa.

Her salt-and-pepper eyebrows went up. "You have a poison dart frog? Isn't that a bit dangerous?"

I shook my head. "He's not toxic. No toxic rainforest bugs in Who's There, Iowa."

"So..." the sister said with a smile, "what were you doing in New Orleans?"

I was probably a little too excited to share as the words gushed out of me. "It was an awesome trip! A friend's husband was arrested for murdering an old dolphin burlesque dancer. I got to mud-wrestle an aged crawdad stripper, fought off the French Whorens while on roller skates and wearing nothing but a bathrobe...oh! And then we had to take on a bunch of alligators in the swamp. One of my friends is really pregnant, so that could've ended badly, but it didn't. And we caught the killer in the end!"

I paused to look out the window. "Wow. The sky looks really

weird. I haven't seen a purple color like that since the time I flew on a mission through Uruguay. That was a strange flight. I had to share it with a dozen chickens, a llama, and a satanic ventriloquist named Ted."

The nun's jaw dropped open. "Why were you on a mission in Uruguay?" After a moment, she brightened. "Are you a missionary, by any chance?"

I laughed. "No. Ex-CIA. I was stalking this terrorist named Rudy...Rudy the Terrorist...which is a really unoriginal name, right?"

The nun's face froze in an expression I could only describe as *Oh no, my toilet is clogged with dead skinks again, and how do they keep getting in there?*—which was something that happened when you spent a weekend in New Guinea.

Or maybe, the look on her face was encouraging me to continue. "Anyway, the case is classified, but let's just say Rudy doesn't live in Uruguay anymore...or anywhere else for that matter."

Sister Cephas looked a little green around the wimple. Oh. Right. Religious people didn't like hearing about things like that. Well, except for that nun in Moldova who was an actual assassin. Sister Olga's hobby often conflicted with her Catholic guilt, so half the time, after taking out a target, she'd try to bring them back to life. It almost never worked.

"Are you okay?" I ventured.

She started. "Oh, yes. I forgot I needed to read this..." she looked around before pulling the airline's magazine out of the pocket in front of her, "...article!"

I squinted at the cover. "The one on emergency in-flight enemas?"

She looked at the cover. "That's right! Always be prepared! That's my motto!"

"Hey!" I grinned. "That's the Girl Scout motto, too! Did you know I'm a Girl Scout leader? I have a great troop!" I paused.

"Well, not right now. I mean, after what they did to my Hitler cat and no-longer poisonous frog...but they're really great kids. Mostly."

Sister Cephas immediately buried her face in the magazine. I guess she really did need to read up on emergency in-flight enemas.

The rest of the flight was uneventful. The nun fell asleep on my shoulder an hour later. Even though I was really nice about waking her when we landed, she didn't even talk to me at the baggage claim. It seemed a little rude.

Imagine my surprise when I walked outside the terminal to see my entire troop, holding a banner that read, WELCOME HOME TO THE BEST LEADER IN THE UNIVERSE!

Rex was with them and immediately took my suitcase. "Welcome home, babe!" He gave me a quick kiss before taking my luggage to the car.

"What's this about?" I asked the girls.

Ava spoke up. As the youngest mayor of Who's There, she often felt the need to speak for the group. "We wanted to welcome you back! That's all!"

"I see," I said with undisguised suspicion. "And it has nothing to do with losing Rufus at the zoo?"

"*Allegedly* lost," Betty said.

"It's not alleged," I pointed out. "I have the whole text stream on my phone. Did you find Rufus?"

Lauren nodded. "Of course we did! And we rescued him from the caiman alligator, too!"

"You should be thanking us for saving his life," one of the Kaitlyns said.

"But you put his life in danger in the first place," I argued.

"That's *your* opinion," Inez said.

"Dr. Wulf called," I began. "She and I think it would be in Rufus's best interest to keep him at the zoo."

The decision was made on my way to the airport. Turned out,

the frog was still at the zoo, so this made everything easier, and he could hang out with his froggy peers. I'd miss him, but Dr. Wulf said I could visit whenever I wanted…within reason. I'm still not sure what she meant by that.

"So we did the right thing," Betty deadpanned.

"Except for him almost being eaten by a small reptile," Lauren added.

"You totally owe us," Inez insisted, "for doing the right thing, even if we didn't know it was the right thing at the time."

I decided to give up. Sister Cephas walked by and flinched when she spotted me. I sketched a wave and turned back to my troop.

"What did you do to that nun?" two Kaitlyns asked, simultaneously.

"I'll bet she tried to throw her off the plane." Betty stared after the woman.

"I did not! She's just tired from a long flight," I insisted.

"Whatever you did," Ava sighed, "I hope you didn't negatively influence a voter."

Rex pulled up in my minivan and hit the automatic door to the rear passenger seat.

"I'm sitting up front with you, aren't I?" I asked with surprise.

The girls started getting into my van. "It's for us," Betty explained. "Well, four of us. The Kaitlyns have their own ride."

Sure enough, the four girls climbed into a car I recognized as belonging to one of their mothers. I got in the van, and Rex headed for the gate.

"This came for you." Inez handed me a piece of mail. "While you were out."

I took it from her. "My mail came to your house?"

"No. Betty took it out of your mailbox," Lauren said.

Rex muttered something under his breath and shook his head.

"It's a felony to mess with the mail," I warned.

Betty shrugged. "Only if you get caught."

I turned toward the backseat. "Stop messing with my mail, or Rex, here, will arrest you. And guess what? I don't think they have Girl Scouts in juvie."

"What's she so mad about?" Ava asked the other girls.

"It's probably that time of the month," Inez replied.

Rex looked at me curiously as if wondering how I was going to handle this.

"Do you even know what that means?" I ventured carefully.

"Not really," Inez admitted.

"Oh good." I sighed. I really didn't want to explain it. When did you have that talk with girls, anyway?

Inez continued. "But my mom says there's a time of the month where a woman gets unreasonably angry, and you have to give her wine and candy or she'll explode."

Inez's mom wasn't far off base. "I'm not unreasonably angry. I simply don't want Betty..." I paused before adding, "or anyone else stealing my mail."

Betty addressed my complaint. "I was just borrowing it. I gave it to you, didn't I? Anyway, I didn't read it, but you should totally take us to that."

"You read it?" I pressed her.

The girl rolled her eyes. "Of course not. But it sounds like fun, and we want to go."

I opened the envelope. Inside was an invitation to our local Girl Scout camp's upcoming Glamping event for adult women. There would be Girl Scout-themed cocktails, s'mores, gourmet food, and use of the ropes course, kayaking, horseback riding, crafts, and the zipline. But this time, it was for adults.

"You can't go," I told the girls as I attempted to hide my excitement. "This is for grownups."

Rex looked hopeful.

"Grownup women," I corrected.

"We're height-challenged, almost-grownup women," Betty said. "Ava's even a mayor."

I only half heard her as I scanned the other side of the invite. "They're going to have cake!" I blurted. "I'm definitely going... and maybe I'll take someone, but it won't be you guys."

The girls complained, but I ignored them and closed my eyes. After the whirlwind trip I just had, I could use a little relaxation under the stars, sitting in front of a fire, eating a dozen s'mores...

...without a single, elderly, mud-wrestling burlesque dancer in sight.

EPILOGUE: FRANKI

TRACI ANDRIGHETTI

"Jim and Kate should be back from that vampire tour." I paced in front of the metal bench in Jackson Square where Bradley sat. "What time is it?"

A corner of his mouth rose. "There's a huge clock right in front of us on the St. Louis Cathedral."

I stopped and stared down at him. "You can't expect me to look at that."

He flashed one of his dazzling smiles. "And why is that?"

"The white Gothic spires look like upside-down fangs."

Bradley took my hand and gazed at me from his seat. "Babe, Jim and Kate are fine. You know how those tours are. They're never on time because they stop and have drinks at a bar."

I wished he hadn't mentioned drinking. Under the circumstances, it didn't make me think of booze.

But blood.

I pulled my hand from his and resumed pacing, careful not to go too close to Mama Esther's table near the end of the square. I was in no mood for her bone business.

"We could go look for them." He shrugged. "Maybe catch the end of the tour."

"Not a chance, Bradley. When I investigated that frat-boy murder, I got my fill of vampires." My fingers went to my throat. *Getting my fill* reminded me of blood-sucking.

"You think you escaped dem bloodsuckers," Mama Esther said, "but they comin'."

The comment was unsettling, but I kept walking. I had no plans to fall prey to whatever doom and gloom the bone-thrower was peddling.

She touched her headwrap. "You can walk away, but it don' change nothin'. I know because I already threw the bones."

Irritation coursed through my blood-filled veins. "Excuse me," I said with a huff, "but that's prying into my personal life."

Bradley raised a brow. "Is it?"

I stiffened. "You're right. That's ridiculous."

Mama Esther's brow shot up. "Is it?"

My curiosity got the best of me, and I was tired of pacing. I pulled out one of the kiddie stools at her table and took a seat.

Her dark eyes roved over the bones. "I see bloodsuckers, and flying, but I cain't tell ya no more dan dat. It's jus' not clear."

All I saw were probable finger digits, but the description sounded like vampire bats. I turned and eyed the gothic bell tower to see whether any of the frightful critters were circling.

"Can you at least tell me if this is going to happen in the Quarter?"

"Unh-uh." She shook her head so hard that her headwrap slipped. "In Iowa."

The blood rushed to my face in anger and embarrassment. "Bloodsuckers in Iowa? Nice try."

I pushed back from the table but two realizations kept me glued to the stool. One, after New Orleans, the second largest community of people who lived as vampires was in Buffalo, which was every bit as random as Iowa. And two, Merry lived in Iowa. She didn't strike me as the bloodsucker type, although she *did* go camping.

My mind wandered down that wooded trail for a moment.

And then pulled back.

No, Merry was normal—mostly.

There had to be another explanation, something I was missing. "Wait. *Camping!* You're seeing *mosquitoes*."

Mama Esther's eyes widened, exposing way too much bloodshot whites for my nerves' liking. "These bloodsuckers are human."

I gripped the table. It was all becoming clear. I was going to fly to Iowa for some reason.

And the bloodsuckers?

Those *Girl Scouts*.

BEHIND THE BOOK

Ciao, *chers*!

Leslie, Arlene, Diana, and I had so much fun writing *4 Sleuths & A Bachelorette* that I thought we should continue the fun by introducing you to each of the Killer Foursome's hometowns. And if any city is synonymous with fun, it's New Orleans where every day is a Mardi Gras party!

Why did we pick burlesque?

Because the title of the first book refers to a bachelorette, we decided to keep the *b* theme going. And burlesque was the first *b* that came to mind in connection with New Orleans. The city has a storied burlesque tradition that continues to this day with the likes of Trixie Minx and Fleur De Tease, a variety burlesque revue sponsored by two of my favorite shops in NOLA, Trashy Diva and Fifi Mahony's (check out their wigs on Facebook or Instagram—you won't believe what you're seeing!).

Anyway, I hope you enjoyed The Big Easy adventure. Oh, and if you want to take a peek at the real-life burlesque dancers who inspired the characters of Caressa and Delphine, search online for the CNN article "Burlesque legends show they've still got it." I dare you to take a peek!

Until the next investigation,
    Traci ~

PREORDER BOOK 3 NOW!

The killer foursome will be back for a third mystery in *4 Sleuths & A Barnstormer*!

Hot on the high heels of a rather strenuous trip to NOLA, Merry invites Valentine, Kate, and Franki to strap on hiking boots in the middle of Iowa for a glamping weekend! Unfortunately, downtime underneath the starry skies, with s'mores and mint-cookie cocktails, turns deadly when an unpopular glamper is murdered.

The suspects seem to outnumber the mosquitos when it turns out nearly everyone bore the victim a grudge. So who did it? One of the wealthy snobs? The trashy drunks? Or the fanatic former scouts?

Go camping with:

Valentine Beaumont ~ Boston sleuth and gutsy beautician

Kate Connolly ~ San Francisco part-time crime-solver and sleep-deprived new mom

Merry Wrath ~ Iowa ex-CIA operative turned Girl Scout leader

Franki Amato ~ New Orleans PI and victim of a serial-matchmaking Sicilian nonna

…and find out who killed the glamper!

ABOUT THE AUTHORS

While you're waiting for *4 Sleuths & A Burlesque Dancer*, catch up on the adventures of each heroine in her own series.

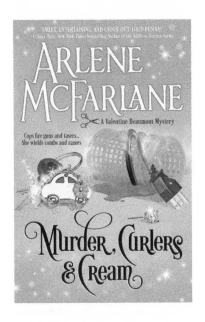

Valentine:

Arlene McFarlane is the *USA Today* bestselling author of the Murder, Curlers series. She's won and placed in over 30 contests, including the Readers' Favorite Book Awards, the Golden Heart®, the Daphne du Maurier, and the Chanticleer International Mystery & Mayhem Book Awards. She's also received a Voice Arts nomination for her audiobook, Murder, Curlers & Cream. Previously an aesthetician, Arlene still dabbles in the beauty industry. She's also an accomplished pianist. When time allows, she plays publicly and posts makeovers on her website. Visit arlenemcfarlane.com/ to learn more!

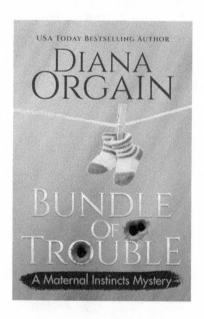

Kate:

Diana Orgain is the *USA Today* bestselling author of the Maternal Instincts Mystery Series. She is also the Author of the Love or Money Mystery series and The Roundup Crew Mysteries (Yappy Hour and Trigger Yappy). Diana is the *New York Times* Bestselling co-author of the Scrapbooking Mystery Series with Laura Childs. To keep up to date with the latest releases visit Diana at dianaorgain.com/.

Merry:

Leslie Langtry is the *USA Today* bestselling author of the Merry Wrath Cozy Comedy series (Merit Badge Murder), the Ukulele Mysteries (Ukulele Murder) and the Greatest Hits dark comedy series—now in development for a TV series ('Scuse Me While I Kill This Guy). Stop by leslielangtry.com/ to find out more!

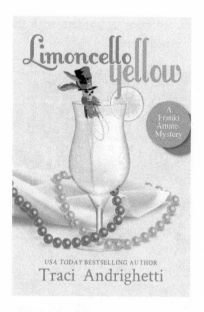

Franki:

Traci Andrighetti is the *USA Today* bestselling author of the Franki Amato mysteries and the Danger Cove Hair Salon mysteries. In her previous life, she was an award-winning literary translator and a Lecturer of Italian at the University of Texas at Austin, where she earned a PhD in Applied Linguistics. But then she got wise and ditched that academic stuff for a life of crime—writing, that is. Get news of Traci's upcoming books and latest capers at traciandrighetti.com.

9 781999 498191